SOLACE

BY

KEVIN TOMASZEWSKI

Solace by Kevin Tomaszewski Published by Edward Tomaszewski

© 2015-2020 Kevin Tomaszewski

Cover by Lucas Bonatto Guerrini

ISBN: 978-0-578-63848-5

DEDICATION

Dedicated to my mother and father for giving me the love and support that fostered my imagination. For my brothers who brought the magic of movies, books and video games into my life that molded my fantasies. For my teachers that developed my love for learning and writing. Finally, for my friends that left an everlasting mark on my life. Each of you all are inspirations, thank you.

TABLE OF CONTENTS

CHAPTER 1
FALL

The air snapped and trembled through the sea of gray clouds above. Alexander pierced through the layers and a lone ray of sunlight shone through where he passed before the cloud cover closed in on itself. His speed kept increasing as he fell, the rushing air muffling his cries of terror. With immense force, he crashed through the forest canopy and slammed into the hard ground, sending dust into the air at impact just as thunder ripped through the air and shook the trees around him.

As the last rumble of thunder rolled into the distance and the man still hadn't moved, the fog displaced by his fall settled back down, covering Alexander. Face down on the ground, the golden glow of a protection spell withered away immediately after impact.

Alexander's skin crawled as the chilly fog rolled over him. The sounds of this place pierced his ears. He gasped and clenched a fistful of dirt before struggling to his feet. A bit unsteady on his feet, he scanned the surroundings and examined his own person for injuries then, in a panic, looked frantically around for his compass. He left the area to expand his search and tripped over an object sticking out of the ground. Upon closer examination, he realized it was a handle. He looked at the handle, up to the sky, and then back to the handle.

Well, could have saved me a lot of trouble if it just hit me.

He grasped the handle and pulled a long blade adorned with ancient markings out of the soil. His search continued until he saw his shield jammed deep into the trunk of a turned-over tree. He wiped the dirt off and looked at the depiction of an eagle with blue and yellow coloring. He secured it, along with the sword, to his person. The search was not over for him, as he continued to wander throughout the area. A sense of urgency rose, and his searching became more and more frantic.

He froze as he spotted a young boy, no older than a toddler, in the shadows of the towering trees outside the impact zone. Dressed in layers of worn, colorless rags, the boy held Alexander's pristine gold compass, which was untouched by the world around him.

Alexander slowly raised a hand to the boy, to gesture that he would not hurt him. But before he could speak a word, the boy turned and ran away into the forest.

"No, wait!" Alexander yelled before giving chase.

As he plowed through the brush, the boy slipped farther into the wilderness. Every time he felt he had closed the gap between them, the boy slipped out of sight. Then Alexander would hear the sound of breaking sticks and he would head in that direction. Eventually he lost sight of the boy going down a hill.

He tripped over a branch and tumbled down, slamming into the base of a tree. Dazed, he looked up to see the boy standing motionless in the middle of a road. Seeing an opportunity, Alexander raced to the boy. He quickly grabbed the compass and was about to scold him for stealing, but was stopped by the sound of grinding metal.

A large metal machine moved toward them. A group of five soldiers, dressed in ragged uniforms, surrounded the vehicle. A lone individual turned around and raised his fist while yelling something to the vehicle over its roar. Black smoke puffed out the back of the machine as it stopped. One of the men approached, while the others raised their weapons at the man and boy.

"You there!" the leading soldier yelled.

Alexander struggled to find the right response to the man's common language. He was finally able to utter a simplistic answer, "Yes?"

"What's your business here? Acropolian? Oren?"

"W-what does that even mean?" Alexander asked, puzzled. He looked at the boy for any insight.

The boy silently returned his gaze.

"It's a simple question, son!" the leader pushed.

"Looks like one of those raiders reported over the radio, sir," one of the other soldiers reported. "Raided those convoys over the last few weeks."

"Probably a scout. Take him out, and the kid!" the leader shouted.

The men aimed their rifles and shot a barrage of bullets. Instinctively, Alexander whipped around his shield to protect the boy and himself. The shield rattled as the bullets hit, while dirt popped around them from the missed shots. Alexander was shocked by the presence of these strange weapons.

Arrows without a bow? Arrows without a stem…at these speeds?

He grabbed the boy and ran to a nearby tree for cover. The soldiers shouted orders as one of them banged on the body of the vehicle. The machine roared to life and a turret appeared from the top to take aim. Alexander glanced around, looking for an escape, but there was none. He sighed, looked at the boy, and held him tight.

"Well, I guess this is one way," he muttered to himself.

An explosion shook the ground and made the boy and Alexander flinch. However, they were unharmed. Instead, the cries and shouts from the soldiers echoed through the air along with the smell of burning metal and flesh.

"Contact left!" one soldier shouted "Right!"

"Where's it coming from?" another soldier frantically yelled.

Alexander looked from behind his cover to see the metal machine engulfed in flames. Two of the soldiers were on the ground motionless, and those who remained looking wildly in all directions. Two snaps rang out, and two more of the soldiers dropped. After the rest of his comrades fell, the last soldier fired in all directions. Alexander noticed that behind the soldier, a shadowy figure dropped from the trees quietly and proceeded toward the unsuspecting soldier. The soldier turned around to see the figure, but was unable to react as it swiped its arm at him. He fell to the ground with his throat slashed, gargling in his own blood until he lay motionless. The shadow revealed itself as a hooded man whose shroud covered his features.

Alexander stood up from behind the tree with his weapons and shield wielded.

"What kind of idiot are you? Put those toys away! Trying to get the kid killed?" The hooded man cursed as he stomped toward the two. Under the hood, the man's face was covered by an armored mask, showing only his mouth and green eyes. The armor was styled to imitate a predatory animal of some kind. His torso was covered in an olive green metallic armor that was worn by dirt, scars, and scuffs.

"I'm not trying to kill anyone; they just attacked us!" Alexander explained to their mysterious savior.

"Don't take me for a fool, guy! I don't care how righteous your cause is; you're not recruiting a child to bring back your lost kingdom!"

"Lost Kingdom? I don't know what you're talking about. The boy just took something of mine and I wanted it back."

Before the hooded man could respond, they were interrupted by the muffled voice from a strange piece of gear off one of the soldiers. It repeated itself over and over, followed by static. The hooded man walked toward the bodies to hear better, then snapped around.

"We have to move, now!" The hooded man urgently directed them down the road in the opposite direction.

"What's going on, what was that?"

"Radio check, every unit is checked by their command regularly. If they don't respond ..."

"What happens?"

"They drop artillery until the area is glass."

"This place is nothing like they said it would be ..."

"Keep your voice down, kid, and move!" the hooded man ordered as the group went off the road into the wilderness.

Chapter 2
Among Shadows

Alexander and his two companions moved throughout the forest for what felt like hours. The absence of sunlight made it almost impossible to tell the time of day. They proceeded with caution with regular stops to check for anything that might be lurking. Finally, they reached a village in a clearing. Huts made from broken stones and rotted wood huddled tightly together.

As they approached the outskirts of the village, the hooded man turned to the boy. "This is yours, yes?"

The boy nodded in agreement.

"Show us your home."

The boy took the lead and guided the two through the village to a small house where a woman was busy repairing the fence. Upon seeing the boy, she dropped her tools and rushed over in excitement.

"Fifle!" She embraced him tightly. "Good to see you've returned. Who are these gentlemen?"

"Dresden, ma'am," the hooded man introduced himself. "This man here is—"

"Alexander," he interrupted quickly.

"Alexander? Such a strange name for this area," the woman observed.

"Yes, it is, isn't it?" Dresden mused.

"Where are you from, sir?" she asked Alexander.

"Well, uhm, ma'am. One could say that I'm not from around here," Alexander replied.

"Yes, I can tell. Your name, dress, and equipment are very odd," the woman replied skeptically.

Alexander scratched the back of his head and struggled to find the right words.

"He came from the sky, Mommy," Fifle piped up suddenly, causing everyone to look at Alexander strangely.

"Well... he's not wrong," he admitted.

The woman's face wrinkled with confusion at the admission and began to guide her son into the house. "We should be getting back inside, looks like it could rain. You gentlemen have a good day."

Dresden gave a salutation to the woman before she closed the door and then turned his focus on Alexander.

"Sky, ay? We should probably get a drink, son," Dresden suggested.

As they passed through the village, Alexander took notice of the conditions. The uneven and unfinished cobblestone streets were filled with mud, littered with scraps and possessed a rotten smell. The people looked destitute as they hobbled along aimlessly to their destinations. Market stands were noticeably empty of the commodities they advertised.

An old woman sitting on the curb stared at Alexander as he walked by. He noticed her emerald-colored eyes, how tired they were against the backdrop of a face wrinkled by the expressions of sadness and hardship she must have endured. He shook his head, feeling a hint of guilt for looking at the destitute condition of these people. It did not help that Alexander stood out among the crowd due to his clothes, which were certainly not clean, but they were more complete than anyone else's. His thick black hair was free of gray. A young, unwrinkled, albeit dirty face with piercing blue eyes was a stark departure from the features of these people. His presence was like a lone candle in a sea of darkness.

A bell tower stood prominently at the town square that had a remarkable scale and artistic style that caught Alexander's eye. He marveled at how the colors that decorated the smooth stone, though faded, made the building shine with prominence. It was almost majestic, and such a stark contrast to the decrepit and depressive state of the rest of the settlement.

Crowds of people gathered around an individual who spoke loudly and boisterously from a cart that elevated him above the crowd. "To what end will these sides go to in order to claim what they call victory in this duel of fates?" the man asked the growing crowd. "Ten years, ten long years since the Long Night descended upon us. In this everlasting night we learned the ultimate truth of where true darkness lies, in the hearts of men. And eight years! Eight years since those accursed farmers discovered those dreadful stones beneath our soil. The miracle of these stones to give us food from the ground…such promise. What was meant to be the foundation of our salvation turned this land into a hellish landscape of blood and ash. As Acropoli and Oren slaughter each other here and tear us apart to save themselves, we must find another place to find our solace."

"Here we go," Dresden muttered.

"As the Goddesses have left us, it is time to look to our past and place our faith in the divine builders, those who transcended reality to

15

become Gods themselves. We at the Harvest Dawn offer you a place to live, safety for your families, food for your stomachs."

Dresden pulled Alexander along. "Come on. I can only listen to so much of this."

"What did he mean by miracle rocks? Oren? Acropoli?"

"I'll explain later."

Dresden gently pushed away a convert who approached, wanting to spread their beliefs, and gestured for Alexander not to lag behind. In the center of the square stood a blue banner that bore an image of a marble column, devoid of any other symbols or text. It was the cleanest object in the entire settlement.

The two arrived at a local tavern called The Armory. The building itself was the remaining piece of a larger structure, modified into a building all its own. Remains of what it used to be a part of were still visible, but were reduced to the foundations that now served as the home for simple tents that housed families of all different sizes. Men and women stumbled out of the tavern in a drunken stupor, the stench of alcohol overwhelming the foul odor that was causing Alexander to gag. In these inebriated villagers, Alexander finally saw a smile.

They entered the tavern and proceeded down a staircase to the lower level which housed a bar. A few patrons sat silently with their drinks. The area was lit by damaged chandeliers, with many of the candles burnt out or missing. They took a seat at the bar; Dresden made a sign for two to the bartender.

"Such a strange name to call a tavern, the Armory, why you think they call it that?" Alexander asked as they received their drinks.

"Because it used to be one. Part of the Maw," Dresden said.

"The Maw Palace? This is the palace of the Kingdom of Termina?"

Dresden took a drink. "It's what's left of the palace... That was destroyed years ago, same with the kingdom."

"Unbelievable," Alexander gasped.

The Kingdom of Termina had a history that many considered legendary due to its resilience. It was commonly known that no matter what disaster ravaged the world, Termina would always survive or, sometimes even come out stronger. Its destruction was a revelation that deeply unsettled Alexander; this was the first place he recognized in a world that caused him such confusion. The fact that this place was now gone only further unnerved the confidence he had of his personal knowledge. In Alexander's mind, there were still a number of different kingdoms peppering the landscape, Termina being one of the more prominent ones. One of the more striking surprises was the presence of such strange weapons that were a horrifying and confusing shock. Although blessed with a number of runes and natural mystical power, he felt his weapons were beyond inadequate for this strange new world.

"So," Dresden started. "You're no rebel. I don't take you for a merchant. Exotic armor, gear that can stop bullets without leaving a scratch. A child's mind is a very imaginative one, but I feel oddly confident in suggesting that you're a Warden."

"The one thing I never thought over before I came down here was how I was going to introduce myself. Didn't really have much time before the jump."

"So, you are claiming to be a Warden, the protectors of old, and all the rest of that mythical stuff?"

"Don't believe me?"

"Does it really matter if you are? From what I know of the old myths, the Wardens left for some reason. Forced us to build new, more

17

deadly weapons to defend ourselves against the monsters and other races that the Wardens used to protect us from," Dresden said.

"Seems like one of those metal chariots could take on a few orcs without much trouble," Alexander suggested.

Dresden smirked a little, "More than just a few. The whole damn race was wiped out by them, among many others. Thanks to our illustrious leaders and their Doctrine of Destiny. Cheers." Dresden sarcastically raised his glass to honor the Doctrine's authors.

"Sounds like some kind of war declaration," Alexander said, frowning into his drink. He ran an index finger around the rim of the glass as if subconsciously looking for something.

"You're on the right path there. It was more like an extermination order. But it brought all the kingdoms together for one of the first times ever. They banded together to make the world safe for humans once and for all. This Doctrine had societies welcome the skill of dwarves, the science of mages, and the intelligence of elves to build new types of weapons and…well a whole new way of life honestly. Guilds were replaced with factories that produced things on a scale never before seen, weapons, metal, bombs, motors, gears, you name it!" Dresden shook his head as he glanced at Alexander. "But I'm sure half the words I just said aren't anything that you would recognize or understand. Of course, I'm guessing this, because you appear as though you don't know shit about this place."

"There are a few gaps in my knowledge, that is accurate," Alexander admitted. "I take it that the Doctrine went well?"

"Oh yeah, real well, that's for sure. Took a few years, but the world was made safe for humans. But, you know what the funny thing is? It turns out that the biggest threat to humans was…well our fellow humans. Not long after we won, everyone just started fighting each other after the sky went dark and folks started losing their minds. Going back to before I went on a rant, what about this jump you mentioned?"

"Well," Alexander started, "It'll sound a little strange, but, the only way to get down here from Skyhold is to be protected by the Goddess' Veil, I guess it would be a spell to you, and then just fall here and hope that the spell doesn't wear off before you hit the ground."

"Huh," Dresden shrugged. "An amusing tale. Friendly advice, though keep that stuff about spells and magic to yourself."

"Why's that?"

"Just trust me," Dresden answered. "After the sky darkened, folks weren't particularly friendly to magic."

"I've answered a few of your questions, how about answering a few of mine?" Dresden nodded and took a few swallows of his drink. "Acropoli and that other one…what was it?"

"Oren."

"That one. Of all the histories I read before coming here, I don't recall those two places being mentioned. And they're warring with each other over what I can assume to be those rocks?"

"Yeah that's about it. Acropoli and Oren are considered the two big players on this part of the continent. Both of 'em grew rich in their own ways. Oren through trade, Acropoli through industry. When, what the prophets call, the Long Night arrived, obviously famine started to become an issue. But, my guess is you wanna know about the rocks. A bunch of farmers here in Termina and the surrounding municipalities somehow were still able to grow their crops with only water and seeds. Folks finally found that a bunch of rocks under the soil that look like marble were the cause."

"Life giving rocks," Alexander commented.

"You know of these?"

"No, haven't ever come across anything like that in my studies. Although geology wasn't a subject I went into in any depth. History is more my interest," Alexander explained, "Still though, a rock that has that kind of power, must be of almost pure essence. Rather remarkable."

"Remarkable is one way to put it," Dresden said, "but deadly is more accurate term. Rocks of Death is a better name for them, but they're officially known as Gaea Stones. Other places like Oren and Acropoli were able to find their own sources, but they had more mouths to feed, and the stones are rather rare. Places caught in the middle of their frantic search became warzones like ole Termina, poor bastards were torn to shreds. Whole cities were even destroyed by the slightest rumor that they had deposits of Gaea under them."

"More right than you know my astute traveler," a man commented as he sat down next to Alexander. "I couldn't help but overhear your conversation about current events."

"Awfully rude to be eavesdropping," Dresden growled, "but I also don't recall inviting you to sit down." Dresden glowered at the man as he made himself comfortable. The man looked like he belonged in academia. Although he was still dirty from his travels, his clothes were much finer than any of the other patrons in the tavern. He removed his feathered cap, combed his fingers through his short black hair, and adjusted his glasses up from the end of his nose. Alexander took particular note of those glasses since he had never seen such things before, only read that some humans needed them to help with imperfect vision.

"It's alright," Alexander turned to the man. "You a merchant of some kind?"

"Heavens no," the man laughed, "but not for my parent's lack of trying. No, no, Doctor Melvin Dixon, adjunct professor of political science at the esteemed University of Soma of the Serene Republic of Oren. At your service, gentlemen."

"Rather impressive line of work, academics is always held in high esteem where I come from."

"And where, my friend, are you from?" Dixon asked with genuine curiosity. Alexander hesitated, so Dresden responded, "From the East, Amber States"

"Ah, the Amber States. Haven't heard much from over there lately. Well, other than rumors, is it true that-"

"We'd rather not talk about it," Dresden interrupted.

"Ah, yes, well, I see, fair enough then."

"Awful dangerous for an academic to be wandering around a warzone. It's common knowledge that this area is pretty fucking bad," Dresden commented.

"Yeah, and I thought I seemed out of place," Alexander added. "What brings you here?"

"Ah, for knowledge of course. This war is perhaps one of the most important debates raging in our government now. Alas, other than the war reports from the military and refugees, there really isn't any actual news coming from here. I aim to change that with some firsthand accounts. I also want to test some of my theories on intrastate conflict on why states fight."

"I think there's a pretty self-explanatory reason for it, friend," Dresden chided.

"Yes, yes, the Gaea Rocks and famine. But it's been eight years and we have, or at least Oren has, enough to feed a great majority of our people. So why does it all continue? That's what I want to answer," Dixon explained to Dresden who only shook his head at the notion.

"So, in your travels, what can you say about the state of this war? I'm not fully familiar with it or the area in general," Alexander inquired.

"Always a pleasure to teach to a person seeking knowledge." Dixon pulled out a small piece of paper and a pen and began to draw a crude map. "This is Varia, of sorts, to the East past the Vola River is, you know, the Amber States and the Twilight Ocean to the West and South. Furthest to the South, on the coast, is Acropoli and their client states. North, past the Nuvian Isthmus is where you'll find Oren and her allies nestled in their own little world of hegemony. We are here, in the middle where Termina is, or was. East of Termina near the Vola is where most of the major fighting is located, but it has died down in recent months. However, the void of government has only proliferated rebel groups, outlaws, armed cults." Dixon glanced at his pocket watch and nodded. "It's about time that I take my leave."

"Late for something?" Dresden asked, suspiciously.

"No not really." Dixon remarked, "I just have a specific amount of time that I like to spend in one place. Not very long, usually, one way to stay a step ahead of the chaos." He gave a small salute before he exited the tavern as quickly as he appeared.

While Dresden consumed his drink as if it were water, Alexander struggled with his as it had a sour smell and an aftertaste that burned all the way down. There was a distinct taste of mushrooms, a food he noticed was a common sight on almost every plate in the tavern.

Dresden could tell by the look on Alexander's face and the way he leaned forward a bit that he wanted to ask a question.

"Go ahead, ask," Dresden sighed.

"The mask, you ever take it off? I see that it's armored so it looks like its protecting you, but it's just so odd," Alexander burst out.

"It's more for protection, I had some injuries a while back that needed some added cover."

"What kind of job would cause such injuries?" Dresden stared silently at his drink for a moment before responding, "Security."

The other patrons of the establishment sat in their own corner, content with their drinks and their portions of mushrooms that they protected from anyone who passed by. Nefarious-looking individuals patrolled about in a search of those who were willing to offer access to extra food, water, or any type of supplies in exchange for various, but broadly defined, work.

Dresden wasted no time in turning one away. A visible blade with a serious look was enough to scare anyone away.

"Now," Dresden looked at Alexander, "the boy said you fell from the sky, and there was an unusually large explosion before you appeared. For all I know, you could have fallen from the sky and are a Warden, or you crawled out from under a rock... It doesn't matter. It's clear that you know nothing about this world."

"My expectations for this world were... different. Last I read, you were all still throwing around swords, spears, catapults and other weaponry. I'm not sure what those soldiers were using or whatever that heinous metal chariot was."

"Soldiers were carrying guns, rifles to be more exact, that can deal a good amount of damage from a safe distance. And that chariot was a

tank, meant to launch a bomb at an enemy from a little further away…
and run over people." Dresden's explanation was cold, as if he saw the
question as elementary. "Of course, swords and other older weapons
still have a use. Outside the army, it's hard to find a rifle…legitimately.
So, there are a number of folks using the stuff that you'd be used to I
suppose."

"Skyhold has nothing close to these kinds of things. Guess our
information about this place is quite out of date."

"Just a little," Dresden grimaced. "Just a little. You're one lost
and uninformed newcomer to these parts. Which begs the ultimate
question," Dresden replied. "Why have you come down from on high?"

"I come... I came to look for someone."

"Someone? A fellow God?"

"We're not Gods... far from it. But, yes, a person I know."

"Well, riddle me this, son. How do you plan to find this missing
friend of yours?"

"With this." Alexander pulled out his compass.

"I've seen compasses before; they usually need a map. Well, unless
of course you come from a magic land where maps might not be
necessary?" Dresden commented.

"Not this one. It's special."

"Of course it is," Dresden quipped.

"It has the ability to point whoever holds it in the direction of their
destiny," Alexander explained.

Alexander handed the compass to Dresden for examination.
The compass went wild in all directions initially before it pointed at
Alexander. Dresden moved his arm around, finding to his bewilderment
that the compass corrected itself to always point at Alexander. His

mind tried to analyze how a compass would focus on a person, it may be a busted compass held by a madman, or maybe Alexander's armor was made of a metal that attracted the needle, or maybe it was magic and his destiny lay with this strange person he just met.

"Where does it tell you to go? If it's showing multiple paths, it means your mind is clouded. Let your mind relax and exhale, that should fix it. Or at least that's what I was told," Alexander said, trying to glance at the compass.

"Nowhere in particular," Dresden said as he gave back the compass. "Guess my destiny is something even the Gods don't know."

"Well, in any case, this compass will get me to the destination. But it doesn't mean it will guarantee success, by any means."

"Well, it sounds like an interesting problem. I also have a developing problem," Dresden admitted. "You."

"Me? What did I—"

"The sound of you *landing* here was louder than anything I ever heard. Probably what triggered that patrol to roam around where they found you, and now they are dead. Luckily, I still had some armor piercer bombs left for that tank. But, it's not hard to believe that more soldiers are going to be searching for their killer, also didn't help that I decided to blow up the damn tank. Then again, they were asking for it for having an exposed fuel tank on the side. Worse, the kingdom is in the middle of full-blown civil war."

"Why is that worse?"

"Everyone is considered suspicious."

"Wh—" They were interrupted by the sound of yelling outside.

CHAPTER 3
WATCH THE FIRE BURN

Terror struck the people as they rushed through the streets in a hapless craze. Dresden and Alexander hurried out of the bar to the sound of screams and the grinding of metal in the distance. The bell tower rang at a furious pace, signaling a warning. The grinding grew louder and louder, overtaking the screams of the terrified masses. Alexander drew his sword and shield while Dresden crouched to the ground to observe the pebbles that shook with the ever-growing noise. Then, the noise stopped. The people stopped. The pebbles stopped. Dresden stood back up.

"What's happening?" Alexander asked.

"Run, as fast as you can," Dresden whispered. "Go!"

A whistle pierced the silence, and then an artillery round struck a nearby building. The two men sprinted down the street as the people ran around in a panic. Explosions struck the area in successive order. As they rounded a corner, an explosion blew out a wall and knocked Alexander to the ground. His shield deflected the larger debris, but the shock deafened him.

Dresden rushed over, pulled Alexander up, and yelled directions in his ringing ears. As Dresden dragged him along, he saw fires, falling debris, and people tripping over the dead who littered the ground.

Another shockwave knocked them down. Alexander turned over and found himself staring into the lifeless eyes of the old woman he saw earlier. In that instant, his hearing returned and all the horrors of what he saw around him were now audible.

Dresden pulled him up again and rushed him forward through town. They ran to the town square where people scattered in a frenzy. Explosions continued to harass the surrounding area as each detonation pushed and funneled the crowds to different paths of escape. An incoming artillery round struck the center of the bell tower, severed the structure, and sent the tower crashing down. The collapse kicked up a cloud of dust that made it impossible to see.

In the chaos, Alexander found himself alone with the sounds of war and cries all around. Once pristine and clean, he was now caked in the dust that lingered in the air. He ran around calling out, trying to find Dresden, but no matter how loud he yelled, his calls disappeared into the debris-filled air. To his shock, Alexander collided with Fifle. Before he could say anything, Fifle ran off and disappeared in the dense cloud. Shadows of people passed by like ghosts, which further disoriented Alexander. Out of the shroud of the debris, Dresden appeared and grabbed Alexander.

"Come on!" he shouted. "Move!"

"To where?"

"Anywhere but here!" Dresden yelled as he quickly scanned the area, "We've got to get out of town."

The two rushed out of the village using their speed rather than sticking to cover, a strategy that doomed many of the inhabitants during the bombardment. As they were about to enter the forest on the outskirts of town, Alexander stopped when the explosions ceased. Dresden ran back to where he was standing.

"What are you doing? Come on!"

"But, the attack stopped." Alexander pointed to the village.

"You haven't seen anything yet, now come on!" Dresden yelled, running into the forest.

When they reached the ridge, Dresden and Alexander had a bird's eye view of the village. Both stayed low to avoid silhouetting themselves. Dresden pulled out a rifle scope to see more clearly. He watched for a few minutes before putting down the scope.

"What's happening down there?" Alexander questioned.

"Well, the soldiers have entered the town and it's... routine," Dresden concluded.

"Routine? What is that supposed to mean?"

Dresden handed the scope to Alexander to have a look for himself. Armed men moved throughout the streets. They guided people to the center of the village, where there were more soldiers and more of those armored machines. Alexander noticed a leader among the soldiers who appeared to berate the people as they flowed in. The man was tall, bald, with a white beard. A scar sliced across his left cheek. Surrounded by a team of soldiers, the leader examined the crowd of people and read out a proclamation from a document he pulled out. The distance made his voice hard to hear, but some of the chilling words carried to Alexander.

"Murder of Acropoli soldiers... capital offense... punishable by death," the leader announced to the crowd.

Alexander realized the gravity of the situation and turned to Dresden. "We have to do something!"

"There's nothing we can do."

"You killed those men."

"Yeah, that was a couple of distracted soldiers," Dresden reminded. "There's practically a company down there."

"There has to be something."

"You can't put out every fire, kid. Every now and then all you can do is watch the fire burn."

Frustrated, Alexander continued to watch the scene that unfolded back in town. The leader had finished his speech and stood for a moment as if to look for anyone who would admit to his or her crimes. He glanced at his watch for a few seconds and then instructed the soldiers to pull five people from the crowd, line them up, and force them to their knees.

"What in the world?" Alexander muttered as he noticed a familiar face among the chosen. The boy. Tears rolled down the boy's face as he looked around aimlessly. He appeared to look right at Alexander through the scope as a metal weapon was placed behind his head. In the blink of an eye, his face exploded as the sound of a crack cut through the air.

Alexander jumped, "No!" he yelped.

Dresden threw him to the ground. "Quiet yourself!"

Alexander tried to collect himself as the cracks continued in successive order to five.

"Why are they doing this?" Alexander frantically questioned, his voice cracking in shock.

Six.

"Who does this?" He pleaded for answers.

Seven ...

Chapter 4
Hard Lessons

A lush forest, the sounds of wildlife, and the comforting embrace of the soft grass all pleasured Alexander's awakening senses. He heard a humming sound in the distance. After looking around, he saw a womanly figure standing near an edge that seemed to overlook land farther out. He walked toward her along a white cobblestone road. The rhythmic humming was delightful and perfectly in tune. A series of marble statues beside the pathway depicted heroic figures in the full glory of battle.

When he reached the clearing, her hums grew louder and the sun grew brighter. To his confusion, his calls to her went unnoticed and she simply continued to hum. As Alexander drew closer to her the sun became brighter and hotter. He struggled to move forward, to see through the intense light of the sun. The heat grew unbearable, but he seemed unable to stop himself from walking toward her. The humming grew louder. Alexander began to scream. He wanted to quit moving forward, and for her to stop humming. He cried, he struggled, but he could not stop the world from pushing him forward to an edge he knew was there.

In an instant, the humming stopped and only dead silence remained. Haunting words echoed through the blinding light, "You should have stayed."

Alexander plunged off the edge toward an endless white below....

***

Alexander awoke in a fright and saw Dresden propped against a tree eating his rations. He welcomed Alexander back. From the direction of town, an eerie silence reigned across the ruins. Alexander saw nothing there, aside from scattered fires in the few remaining buildings.

"They're gone?" Alexander asked.

"Left a few hours ago, after they finished mopping up."

"Is there—"

"No one is alive down there. Unless some are still hiding," Dresden interrupted. "In any case, we have to go down there, gather supplies from whatever we can find."

"You want to steal from the dead?"

"The dead don't need anything."

Dresden led Alexander back down to the village. The fires raging throughout the village heated the cold air. Embers floated aimlessly from the infernos that still engulfed many of the buildings. Alexander marveled at how such a large collection of people and places could be destroyed in a matter of hours. Every few minutes brought the sound of another structure collapsing in the distance.

Not a soul was on the streets. It was not until they reached the town square that they found the inhabitants. A sea of bodies littered the ground and the stench was so heavy the air felt thick, making each breath difficult. Most of the bell tower was scattered across the square, and what remained of the lower part of the building was engulfed in flames.

A blue banner with the column symbol still stood in the center of the square with a message posted at the bottom that read: *For the murder of Acropoli soldiers, the king has sentenced this settlement to the death penalty. No one is authorized to build, live, or trade on these grounds. Violators will be tried under capital charges.*

Guilt overcame Alexander after he read the message.

"I did this," Alexander said.

"No, *I* did this," Dresden corrected coldly. "Those soldiers died by my hand."

"But if it wasn't for me, you wouldn't have had to do it."

"Maybe, but doesn't look like it matters now," Dresden said. "You've never seen death before, have you?"

"Death, yes." Alexander wiped away tears that formed as he looked upon the scene. "But never so much of it at once."

"Well, better get used to it. Not like the paradise you fell from." Dresden kicked over a corpse. "You would be better served to take someone's clothing to cover up your *sky fashion*; it'll draw less attention."

A man laid on his back, sprawled out in an awkward pose. The dead man's brown eyes lifelessly stared at Alexander, which caused him to shudder. "I... I don't know if I can do it."

"Unless you want to stick out and be chased from here to The Abyss, you'll do as I suggest."

"Doesn't sound like a suggestion."

"It is a suggestion; it's just one with no other choices to pick from," Dresden sarcastically joked while he continued to rummage through the bodies.

Alexander looked around his surroundings at the mangled corpses, the desolate crumbled buildings, and the fires. "No!" Alexander objected.

Dresden dropped what he was doing and stormed over to Alexander. "Listen to me, son! If you want to die, then keep your stupid sense of morality and sorrow for the dead. If you care for the dead, then you will become one. Alternatively, you can do what is necessary to stay alive. Which is it going to be?"

Alexander was silent and glanced around again.

"Go ahead and make your choice. Once I get what I need, I'll be gone," Dresden said before he went back to his business.

Alexander pondered in the cold silence. A breeze swirled the embers from the building fires. He took a deep breath and began to search the bodies. He removed several articles of clothing from the corpses to cover up his armor and weaponry. Dresden walked over to Alexander, who was still searching bodies, and threw a handful of mud in his face.

"Clean means death," Dresden muttered as he continued to the surrounding buildings to search for salvageable gear.

Alexander tried to clean the thickest parts of mud off his face. He noticed a food cart at the other end of the square and decided to check it for anything he could eat. As he stepped over corpse after corpse, the sweat on his face mixed with the mud and dripped into his eyes, causing a burning sensation. His attempt to wipe his eyes caused him to trip and fall to the ground. He found himself face to face with the lifeless eyes of Fifle and what remained of his face. Silently, he stared deeper into the boy's dead eyes. Alexander's fists clenched the ground and grew tighter the more he looked at the boy. He wasn't released from this trance until Dresden kicked him to his feet.

"Was able to find some food we can cook later on. The rest of the food here is spoiled beyond consumption." Dresden looked at the child's body. "You know, it's funny. If I had just let you two die on that road, then this whole place would not have been destroyed. Now, all I have left from that decision is you. Sure hope you were worth it."

Alexander picked himself up. "I am sorry for this, all of this. I caused this. They never told me it was like this down here."

"Best learn as you go. Nothing in this world is immortal, no man, no myths, not even the stars above."

"No. I can very well see that the Gods left this place long ago."

"Where does your compass tell us to go now?" Dresden asked.

"Us?"

"Yes, us," Dresden responded. "Saving your ass cost the lives of this entire town. I can only hope to salvage something here by seeing that you accomplish your little task."

"Thank you."

"Don't thank me. I'd have left you on the road if I could go back."

"Oh."

"But, since I can't…" Dresden stopped in thought. "I hope you're worth it."

Chapter 5
They Burn the Clothes

For hours, the two traversed the bleak wilderness, avoiding trails and signs of activity. The path of most resistance was taken at every turn at Dresden's guidance. Every few hundred meters, Alexander stopped to correct his direction. He soon became frustrated by Dresden's insistence at going through the more difficult terrain; up and around cliffs, over rocks as big as buildings, and over logs as large as the biggest beasts known.

"You're adding who knows how long to this journey by having us go through such awful terrain!" Alexander protested.

"It's safer this way."

"Safe," Alexander jested. "Tell me what is safe about being a misstep away from certain death upon a wet cliff?"

"The man who fell from the sky is afraid of heights," Dresden said under his breath. "Certain death is always a misstep away. Out here, you don't want to run into any soldiers or others wandering about."

"Others? Like who?"

"There are worse things than soldiers or bandits out here."

"Be that as it may, these constant corrections aren't going to get us to where we need to go in my lifetime. Even this compass is getting me turned around at this point."

Dresden leaned against a tree and crossed his arms. "Well, maybe some more details about your destination would help. A name? Description?"

Alexander thought for a moment as he examined the compass. "When I was given this compass I was told, 'Go to where the first brick was laid in the Crescent Valley. Where man and Gods are now dust and echoes.'"

"Interesting, a riddle. Just my luck."

"Supposedly, it was where the Eagle last rested. That part confused me the most, but I assumed I would be guided better down here. I was always taught that the Empire of Roads connected all corners of the land."

"At one time, perhaps, well before my time. I was once told that they were all paved with the smoothest of stones and marble. But, after everything went wrong, people either avoided the roads because of bandits or they were stripped for scrap to repair buildings."

"Well, I guess the option we have is to keep walking until my compass stops pointing," Alexander surmised.

"Land navigation is more than just a compass and an ambiguous description of a destination. A seasoned traveler could probably go off it, but neither you nor I have the knowledge to do it."

"I would have assumed you were a man of the woods."

"I am not."

"What are you then?"

"Not important," Dresden sighed. "Unfortunately, I think we are going to need a map."

"Ah, good, a map would make this a little better. What market should we go to for one?"

Dresden shook his head. "Not that easy. Maps are a rarity these days, mostly due to the fact that they are illegal to possess if you are a civilian."

"Outlawing maps?"

"Oh, yes, they can be used by anyone who would want to fight the government. Rebels mostly. It's funny, really, the people who would use them the most are those who just want to get out of the way of everything that wants to kill them. It's harder since every criminal finds a way to get them and use them for raiding," Dresden explained.

"So, how do we go about getting one? From the criminals?"

For some time they discussed different plans about how to obtain a map. Neither of them knew exactly what to do. Dresden knew time was short and that patrols, bandits, or other hostile forces were sure to come at some point. He decided that the best chance they had was to skirt along the nearest road to the next town and sort it out from there.

As the two set out in their new direction, they redoubled their attention as the crackling thunder of artillery began again in the distance. Although the sound meant trouble could be coming, the loud booms helped mask the crunching of dead leaves underfoot. The wind picked up again, making the forest seem alive with the whisperings of vanished life. Rain drizzled from the sky periodically, making the ground more difficult to navigate.

Dresden raised his fist to signal halt and sniffed the air from under his armored mask. Alexander caught a pleasant scent in the air. The food of some kind was being cooked which could mean anything from a settlement to a military encampment.

"Where is that heavenly smell coming from?" Alexander wondered.

"Don't know, must be nearby. We got to get a fix on it so we don't end up stumbling into someone we don't want to meet."

They proceeded to a nearby hill that looked as though it would give a good vantage point of the area. Alexander reached the top of the hill first and began to look around for the source of the smell. Dresden pulled Alexander to the ground and put his hand over his mouth. He silently pointed to the other side that had a clear view of a light in the distant field.

Dresden pulled out his riflescope to get a better look, then sighed.

"Well? What is it?" Alexander said impatiently.

"Roamers," Dresden grumbled as he handed Alexander the scope.

"Who are they?"

"People you don't want to meet, ever."

Alexander examined the scene before him for a minute as Dresden pulled out a piece of bread to eat.

"Well, whoever they are, they are eating better than us."

"Depends on your taste."

About seven individuals dressed in a mixture of different clothing styles stood around a fire pit cooking a piece of meat. Alexander tried to remember all the encyclopedias he'd read on the creatures of this world as he pondered what kind of beast it was. His inquisitive face turned still and pale as a chill overcame his senses. Alexander shuddered at his realization and before he could utter a word he dropped the scope and gagged violently. Dresden calmly retrieved the scope, wiped it clean, and put it away.

"You all right?"

"How are they... how are you so calm about this? That's a person they're eating there," Alexander whispered through his tears as he wiped away the vomit, "and from the size of the body it looks no bigger than a toddler."

"See it enough times and it stops affecting you, eventually. Still disgusts me, but never shocks anymore. All you can do is shrug it off and move on. It's strange though, this time."

"Oh, there is something *strange* about it just this time?"

"They normally don't use the clothes as fuel for the fire. The wood must not be good enough anymore. We need to keep moving."

The two traveled for hours without a stop. Dresden emphasized the importance of putting as much distance as possible between themselves and the Roamers anytime Alexander asked for a break. They were a different kind of people, the Roamers, without a flag or any purpose other than survival. Dresden informed him that the people who became Roamers were usually the weaker-willed individuals who voluntarily abandoned their basic morality in order to stay alive. Rather than choosing a sense of humanity, these people adopted a nature similar to animals, but with the cunning thoughts of a seasoned sociopath. Eating other people was only a small part of their savage nature. These revelations were enough to keep Alexander moving, despite his exhaustion.

Dresden glanced up at the never-ending sea of clouds and said, "Hm, looks like rain."

"Oh yeah, sure. It looks like rain," Alexander found it laughable at how one could tell what the weather might produce in this dark, dreary world.

A rainstorm unleashed itself as the two traversed down a steep hill to the surprise of the out of place Warden. The torrent turned the ground into a muddy mess that made each step more difficult than the last. Alexander lost his footing and began to slide down the hill uncontrollably. Dresden was trying to grab a tree to avoid falling and missed catching Alexander as he slid past. Alexander bounced off rocks and trees as he tumbled to the bottom. He coughed when he landed, doubling over in pain. Effortlessly, Dresden reached the bottom in a controlled slide that left him standing without injury.

"Can we rest now?" Alexander asked miserably.

"Sure, we can stay there." Dresden pointed to the ruins of a massive castle that lay before them.

"Creepy decrepit castle, great."

"We can keep walking," Dresden suggested as he helped Alexander up.

"No, nope, this'll do."

The inside of the castle was as haunting as the outside with the shells of barren and ghostly rooms and corridors littered with structural debris. The walls bore the scars of an inferno.

The two went deeper into the castle to find a room that wasn't exposed to the severe weather outside. As they proceeded, Dresden noticed the place was littered with spent bullet casings, arrows, swords and various other weapons. The walls were peppered with bullet holes and large holes from apparent explosions. In one instance, the two found an unexploded artillery shell that had pierced several floors before reaching the ground floor.

"What kind of weapon is that?" Alexander asked, pointing.

"The kind that can take out a good part of this place. Should consider ourselves lucky."

Farther down the hall, barricades bore the scars of heavy damage. Along the walls behind the barricades were considerable amounts of bullet holes. Unlike the endless nature of other corridors, this one was a dead end.

"Last stand. Must have been one hell of a fight," Alexander suggested.

"Seems that way, doesn't it?" Dresden carefully examined the area behind the barricades.

"What's got your interest?"

"The defenders' weapons."

"What about them?"

"They had none."

"Come again?"

"All the other halls are littered with weapons, presumably by the fallen who tried to rush this area. Doesn't seem to be any beyond here. Also, there weren't any bullet holes at the other end, so they didn't use rifles."

"Find that hard to believe. They had to have swords or something." Alexander leaned up against the wall to rest. The wall gave way to reveal a hidden room.

The two looked at each other. "Should we?" Alexander asked.

"Might as well."

The hidden room was filled with tables littered with papers and scientific instruments. Vials, scales, and containers were scattered about the tables and the floor. Bookshelves were overturned or broken with all their contents piled up like garbage.

Dresden examined one table that had a mountain of papers with sketches and descriptions. Dead plants and herbs on the table led him to conclude, "Mages."

"Mages? Why would mages be targeted like this?"

"They fell out of favor after the sky went dark. Every kingdom turned their forces against them, probably the last act of unity we had in this land before everyone turned on each other."

"What would make people believe the mages caused the sky to go dark?"

"They were different; that's the only crime they really committed."

"So, all of them were hunted down?"

"And exterminated."

"That's madness!"

"Indeed, especially when considering that the mages were the ones who advanced our civilization's technologies with their research. Gave the world the weapons needed to fight the myths after you Wardens left," Dresden explained. "Tragic that these people were killed by the very weapons they helped create."

"So there really aren't any left?"

"Well, enormous effort was put into finding them. Some even had technology that could track them through the magic remnants left behind. All sides really wanted them dead."

Alexander glanced through some of the books. "From these books, this mage in particular had an interest in the underworld. A big interest," Alexander noted with curiosity as Dresden walked around the room. The floor was covered by torn-out pages covered with edits and drawings of symbols. Under the papers, Dresden noticed something unusual on the floor.

"Yeah, I guess I would too if I was in their position," Dresden commented as he uncovered a large star on the floor that had various symbols painted on it. It was the same symbol seen in many of the books about the underworld. "Of course, this one must have been interested for other reasons."

"Why? What is that?"

"The mark of The Abyss. Nut jobs and their black magic. Who knows what this one was trying to do," Dresden said.

"The Abyss, so it is," Alexander concluded as he touched one of the vials filled with a green liquid. He jerked his hand away. "Warm."

Dresden looked over. "What?"

"The vial is warm," Alexander said just as he noticed that a nearby candle had wet wax sitting around the wick.

"We're leaving, now!" Dresden ordered.

"Don't have to tell me twice."

CHAPTER 6
THE MIRACLE WORKER

As they continued their journey, the two smelled an aroma that made their mouths water. The scent of cooked meat made Dresden cautious, as he feared it could be another group of Roamers nearby. Stricken with hunger and low on food supplies, the two went in search of the source. The trail proved fruitful for the two travelers.

Behind the cover of the wood line, they found a village tucked away in the vast wilderness. No road led to the village, which struck Dresden as odd, since the roads, although full of hazards, acted as the lifeblood of a settlement. No matter how perilous the risk, no civilized community isolated itself from the ancient roadways that crisscrossed the land.

The village itself was a congregation of simple huts made of mud with straw roofs, but there was something off about the place. These villagers were not destitute, and they seemed happy. Alexander did not miss the surprisingly positive mood and wondered whether the whole thing was an illusion.

"What do you think they're cooking?" Alexander asked.

"Smells like meat, which makes me nervous," Dresden commented. "They don't look much like cannibals though."

"Try not to judge too much on appearances. That'll usually be the last mistake you'll make," Dresden grunted.

They hesitated to enter the village at first, but they were low on food and the heavenly smell that emanated from the camp was too good to resist. After a moment of discussion, the two men walked out of the woods into the camp.

To their surprise, the villagers that greeted them were inebriated and cheerfully welcomed the strangers into their settlement. After entering the center of the village, it came as no surprise why a good many were drunk. The decorations and food were signs of a festival.

"Flowers, they actually have flowers," Alexander noticed.

"More importantly," Dresden gestured to the table of seemingly endless food, "They have food."

The source of the attractive smell was, in fact, food. However, it was not the usual mushrooms or other foods that grew in the darkness, but food that had not been seen since the sky went dark. On a banquet table were leftovers of cabbage, carrots, potatoes, endless loaves of bread, fruits of various kinds, and fat game.

Wide-eyed and speechless, the two stood before the table and wondered what to do. Alexander was the first one to break as he began to gorge himself on whatever food he could touch. Dresden, after an initial hesitation, grabbed the nearest meat and proceeded to sample every different roasted animal. Distracted by the sensation of exotic nourishment, the two did not notice a group of villagers surround them. When they finally did notice they were being watched, they stopped in embarrassment and tried to apologize for their rude behavior.

The leader of the village stopped their fumbled overtures and offered them a smile. "Friends, friends, please don't stop eating," the man said with a laugh. "You're more than welcome to our food. But I am sorry to say that you missed the party."

"Thank you, sir," Alexander said.

"Yeah, looks like a good time," Dresden commented.

"Indeed, it was, strangers. My name is Herald Boran, mayor of our humble village. What are your names?"

"Alexander."

"Dresden."

"Well, Alexander and Dresden, welcome to Solace," Herald said. "Please feel free to eat, drink, rest, whatever."

"We appreciate the kindness, sir." Dresden thanked.

"Herald, please," he insisted. "What brings you this far out in the forest?"

"We're just travelers trying to stay a step ahead of the chaos," Dresden said.

"A good idea. Pretty bad out there," Herald said as he joined them at the table. "You're not bringing any of it this way, are you?"

"No, we've been staying ahead of it pretty well," Alexander responded.

"Oh, good."

"Get much trouble out here?" Alexander asked.

"No, we haven't had any problems out here for a while now," Herald informed them.

"All right, I'll ask," Dresden interjected. "The food—"

"Where did it come from?" Herald finished.

"Yes."

"Was wondering when you might ask about that," Herald admitted. "I want to say that it's complicated, but it isn't."

"I would say that unless you got yourself a miracle worker, then it probably will be pretty complicated," Dresden commented.

Herald simply smiled and fiddled with a piece of bread. "Well, we have a good Warden."

"You have a what?" Alexander asked as he stopped mid-chew.

"We have a Warden," Herald reiterated with a cheery laugh.

The travelers looked at each other blankly.

"If you want, I can take you to meet her," Herald offered.

"Her?" they responded simultaneously.

Dresden turned to Alexander. "Alex, this might be it."

"I'm not so sure about that."

"Not going to find many Wardens down here, much less a female one. Go check it out. I'll take a look around the place," Dresden urged.

"All right, I'll take a look," Alexander agreed. "Sir, I would love to meet your Warden."

"Excellent, I'm sure she'll be thrilled to meet you!"

Herald led Alexander to meet their Warden. The path took them outside of town into the woods. As they went deeper, Alexander noticed that the plant life changed from a dead gray to a rich green. The vibrant-colored flowers were in full bloom and a stark contrast to what Alexander had seen in his travels. Trees were full of leaves, insects crawled or flew around, and wild animals were all around them. This paradise was filled with a sense of something sacred that excited the senses.

"You admire the home our Warden made?" Herald asked.

"It is quite the sight," Alexander said. "Almost seems impossible."

"Impossible is no obstacle to her. She cured every ailment we suffered. She gave water to quench our thirst, food for our hunger, and cures to our diseases," Herald praised.

"I look forward to meeting this Warden."

Herald led him to a simple log cabin between two towering oak trees that housed a chorus of birds singing a hypnotic tune. He knocked at the door and a voice welcomed him in. Inside, Alexander was introduced to the slender, brown-haired woman who'd worked the miracles. Her emerald-green eyes sparkled, and she wore a colorful gown decorated with flowers that gradually changed colors from blue to yellow to red to purple and a few other colors.

"Dear Julia, we have a visitor who would like to meet you," Herald told her.

"Herald, so good to see you!" Julia greeted him. "Yes, of course, always happy to meet new people. Who might you be?"

"My name is Alexander."

"A fine name. What brings you here?"

"The food, initially, but I'm told you're a Warden?" Alexander asked.

"Ah," she said. "Herald, thank you, but would you be able to give us a moment?"

"Of course, Julia. Tonight still on?" Herald asked.

"Absolutely it is," she said.

Herald left the cabin and the two were alone. Alexander took a hard look at the room's interior. Makeshift dreamcatchers adorned the walls along with paintings of exotic landscapes. Bookshelves filled with books on various subjects from magic to the occult were interrupted by the occasional candle or exotic stuffed bird. Around the room were various pieces of equipment that Alexander didn't recognize, but then he realized what he was looking at.

"You're no Warden," Alexander claimed.

"Well, of course I am, Alex… mind if I call you Alex?"

"Sure."

"Well, Alex, I am the Warden of this town; at least that's what the villagers call me." She looked at him inquisitively. "Wait, you don't mean the whole…" She gestured to the sky. "Oh, don't be silly."

"I do mean that. It was a curious thing to me, because the things I assume that you've done for these people and this area are not things I've seen from a Warden."

"*Seen* from a Warden? Where have you seen a Warden?" she asked in a humorous tone until she noticed Alexander's straight face, "Wait. No."

Julia rushed to a chest and rummaged through its contents. After she threw out a number of things, she grabbed a jar that contained a mysterious powder. She opened it up, grabbed a fistful of the powder and approached Alexander. "If you really are," Julia said as she tossed the powder into the air. The powder lingered in the air for a moment before the specs of powder began to vibrate together as if searching for something. Alexander, unsure of what was happening, took a step back. As he stepped back, the powder hovered closer to him. Now unnerved by this reaction, he took another slow step only to be consumed by the cloud of powder that attached itself to his cloak. A moment of panic overcame Alexander as he coughed from breathing in some of the substance while he furiously wiped it off himself. She gasped at the reaction and gestured for him to calm down.

"What the hell is this stuff!" Alexander said in a panic.
"Don't worry, don't worry, its harmless," Julia tried to say with ease but was unable to contain her excitement.

"Oh, I thought I was going crazy when I sensed a large amount of Essence. But, it was you… you're pulsing with Essence!"

"And you're not?" Alexander gestured all around. "I assume you use it to make all these *miracles* happen?"

"Oh no, don't be ridiculous. I'm just an ordinary mage. I can only manipulate it. You, though, are full of it. You are a Warden!"

"I am," Alexander said.

"Hasn't been a Warden in…" She paused. "Doesn't matter. What are you doing here?"

"I'm looking for someone, another Warden," Alexander explained.

"Another Warden? There's another one here?"

"Well, not exactly," Alexander explained. "She's dead."

"A dead woman, you say?" Julia rubbed her chin. "A resurrection."

"Not a resurrection," Alexander corrected. "I just want to bring her back from—"

"Taking a soul from The Abyss is a resurrection no matter what way you spin it, Alex. But, never mind that. So, you are looking for a way to get into the land of the dead to rescue your friend. Interesting. How did you plan on getting there?"

"There's a place here that serves as the natural gateway to The Abyss; at least that's what I was told before coming here. But everything I read about this place appears to be wrong, so I don't know if all that could be out of date now."

"Hm, a natural gateway. I'm not entirely familiar with one, but if there is, I'm sure it's caked in so much allegory and conjecture that it will be a rather fun riddle to unravel. Could open a gateway manually, but that can only be done with the blackest of magic, and only pure Essence. Of course, everything you have is pure Essence, considering your origin."

"I'm not looking to use any nefarious magic; nothing good can come from that," Alexander protested.

"Oh no, you would never be able to. Wouldn't know the first thing to do when it comes to opening a door to the underworld. The path one would have to take to get that ability would corrupt you beyond redemption."

"Well," he recalled, "I ran across a lab where another mage appeared to be exploring that path pretty intently."

"Not at all surprising. After the kingdoms of Varia launched a genocide against anyone who wielded Essence or knew a spell, many of us turned to the dark arts to fight back. That just ended up killing them, too."

"I see you survived."

"Not without great effort, I assure you," she quipped, "Not many were able to do the things I had to in order to make it this far."

"If the people turned against you all, why are you so openly living in a village and helping its people?"

"Well, I got sick of the whole hermit lifestyle. Technically, I still am a hermit, since I live isolated from the rest of them, but it's better with others. Since there aren't really other mages around, might as well make friends with regular people."

"Aren't you afraid of getting reported?"

"Report me? Hah! Look around, I give them all their desires and cure their illnesses. I protect them from the harsh reality that plagues the rest of the world. I'm like a God to them!" Julia proclaimed.

"Yes, they do seem pretty fond of you."

"And I them. Of course, I'm boasting about the *God* nonsense. I'm just as susceptible to a sword or bullet," Julia said. "Hm, I actually can help you though, Alex."

"Help in what way?"

"Well, I can't open a gateway to The Abyss, but I can probably let you have a conversation with your friend. A little commune is harmless."

"Talk to her?" Alexander asked in disbelief. "You can do that?"

"Indeed, I can. One of the few spells I know that has a slight shade of dark, but really isn't. Talking to the dead is definitely not as serious as necromancy."

"What would I have to do?"

"Nothing really, just take a seat and we can get started."

"Why are you doing this? I just met you, and you want to help me?"

"It's not every day that a Warden strolls through. This world can use the Wardens, and if you're here to bring another back, then I'll give you a hand in your journey," Julia explained.

"Thank you, Julia."

CHAPTER 7
DEAD MESSENGER

Julia pulled a chair out for Alexander and then rushed around to gather a bunch of different materials and set them up in a circle around him. Candles were set up and lit and skulls were placed strategically on the perimeter while the rest of the circle was outlined by salt. Julia altered the design that bore a striking resemblance to the figure Alexander saw in the abandoned castle. It gave him pause, and he became uncomfortable by her design, and this discomfort was not lost on Julia. The discomfort was increased once Julia grabbed a rabbit and prepared to sacrifice it in the center of circle.

"I said I don't want black magic, blood magic, dark magic, whatever!" Alexander yelled.

"Relax," she consoled him. "You only really get into the dark stuff if we start using humans as sacrifice. Now there is a small catch I should mention before we get started for real."

"What?"

"Only the purest of Essence can be used to open a line to the underworld. So, this bunny has to be sacrificed by your hand."

"Absolutely not!"

"Listen, we all have had to make a life out of doing things that make us uncomfortable in order to get what we want. I can't tell you what I've had to do to stay alive," Julia explained

After a moment of thought, Alexander relented and took hold of the rabbit. Julia gave him a dagger to complete the ritual, but instructed him to kill the rabbit after she recited the necessary chants for the spell to start. She closed her eyes and began a hypnotic chant in a mysterious language. She gave a subtle signal to Alexander to kill the rabbit. Hesitating at first, he cut the rabbit after Julia made another signal and the blood poured into the middle of the design. When the blood hit the floor, a light rippled out through the salt outline. Julia continued her chants as the room began to shake and the light darkened. The vibrations intensified to a violent tremor that escalated to a point where Alexander feared the cabin would collapse. In an instant, the tremors stopped and an ominous orb of white light rose from the blood of the sacrificed rabbit.

"What's your friend's name?" Julia asked.
The Warden gazed at the ground in silence. Julia lowered her head to put herself in his view with her eyebrows raised in anticipation of his answer. Alexander caught her gaze and sighed, "Emily."

"Took a while for you to remember? You sure she was that important?" Julia suggested.

"Yes, she was, is!" he yelled, to Julie's surprise.

"Well, alright now, my apologies. She died recently?" Julia asked Alexander, who nodded in agreement. "We seek the soul of the recently deceased Warden formerly called Emily."

Julia's announcement echoed in the orb as it acted as a conduit to the underworld. It flickered in response whenever she spoke to it.

She continued to call for the soul of Emily, but there was no answer. Alexander started to become restless at the silence.

"Why isn't it working?" he asked impatiently.

"The Abyss is a pretty crowded place. Give it a moment." She turned back to the orb. "Emily, I have Alexander with me. He wants to talk to you."

The orb flickered and echoed the announcement until it lowered to a whisper. A loud chime emanated from the orb, signaling that a connection had been made. The orb's color changed to a cloudy blue as the sound of a gale force wind traveled the course of the connection. When it reached its destination, the wind stopped and a rich purple glowed from the orb. The air warmed, and a sense of comfort filled the room and left him speechless.

"Are you there, Emily?" Julia asked.

"Who's there?" a soothing, yet haunting voice echoed from the orb.

"That's her! Emily!" Alexander shouted in disbelief.

"Alex? Is that you?" Emily asked in a nervous tone.

"Yes! Yes, it's me, I'm here."

"Where? I don't see you. I don't see anything. I can't see!"

"Alex, careful, I'm not sure what kind of state she is in. No one really knows what it's like to be dead, remember," Julia advised.

"Alex, who else is there?" Emily asked.

"A friend. She made it possible for us to talk right now," Alexander explained. "I can't tell you how good it is to hear your voice."

"Where are you? I still can't see."

"I'm…" Alexander paused, not knowing how to explain. "I'm on my way to get you. I'm gonna bring you back."

"Bring me back?"

"Yes, bring you back to life," Alexander said.

The orb changed when he made that announcement. The color began to lose its purple glow and darken to black. An ominous gurgle churned out of the orb and Julia began to get nervous.

"Easy with the whole resurrection thing, Alex. She might be talking to you, but I'm sure the entire damn underworld is listening, including its custodian," Julia warned.

"They don't like it?"

"Saying that you're trying to break the cycle of nature is probably going to ruffle some feathers," Julia explained. "Wait a minute."

Julia grabbed her head to concentrate on something that troubled her. The orb continued to turn pitch black and the room lost its warmth. The windows began to frost as a frigid cold overtook the room. Comfort had been replaced by an intense feeling of tension.

"Someone else is tapping in. Not from below; it's local."

"Who?"

"Someone, someone who… we have to stop."

The orb sent out a shockwave that knocked them both on their backs. The windows shattered and the salt blew away, revealing an outline of light that drew out the design.

"*Warden*," a haunting voice called from the orb.

"Who is that, Julia?" Alexander asked nervously.

"Whoever is listening," Julia replied with a distressed expression that turned her face pale as snow. That distress turned to horror as whatever was listening appeared to have an impact on her senses.

"Alex?" Emily called out in fright.

"Emily, I'm still here."

"Alex? I'm scared. You shouldn't have done this," Emily said.

"*Such childish need,*" the voice judged.

"Emily, I'm coming for you! You hear me? I'm coming!" Alexander yelled.

"There's so much. You should have stayed," Emily said.

Before Alexander could react, the orb imploded and the light faded away. Hearing those ominous last words sent a chill up Alexander's spine. Julia simply stared at him and waited for a reaction of some kind.

"Emily?" Alexander called helplessly to where the orb once was. "Emily!" Alexander, in a fit of rage, slammed his fists on a nearby table with such force that it snapped in half. As sudden as his rage boiled over, Alexander calmed down and realized what he had done. To be so close to her again, his mind numbed from the experience of losing her again.

"Who was that?" Alexander asked.

"Someone who knows you're here. And might be looking for you now," Julia said. "You need to leave."

"Right now?"

"Yes, whoever that was... all I felt was hate. All of it was so strong and so corrupted." Julia paused. "We might have attracted attention that you really don't want. Clearly, this *person* has enough time and power to commune with The Abyss constantly. Since I doubt that the person is just sightseeing... you just need to leave."

"What about you? Whoever that was might come here first."

"Oh, I'll be fine. Been in tougher scrapes before," Julia reassured him. "You just go."

Dresden kicked in the door of the cabin, which caused the two to jump in fright.

"What the hell is going on in here?" Dresden demanded as he examined the room.

"This is Julia; she's a mage, not a Warden," Alexander explained.

"Yeah, I got that. What the hell is with all of this?" He pointed to the remains of the setup for the spell.

"Julia was trying to help enchant my compass so it could lead us away from danger while keeping us on the right track," Alexander explained as he glared at Julia.

"Well, did it work?"

"Not really. I'm not that skilled with enchanting anything other than simple things in nature," Julia covered for him.

"Guess that would explain the stuff in the village. A spell like that caused that loud explosion?"

"Like I said, I'm rusty," Julia said.

"Well, in any case, we should probably get back to our travels," Alexander advised.

"Nonsense, the day is almost over. Herald said we could stay the night. We can get some good rest and start out fresh tomorrow."

Unable to come up with an excuse to counter Dresden, Alexander relented. Julia suggested they stay, as well, and quietly reassured Alexander that they should be safe here for the night. He knew that she was probably saying that to keep him calm, but he let himself believe the potential lie. They were taken back to town and set up in a hut for the night.

As night fell on the town the people went off to sleep. There were no guards, no patrols, no one watching the forests for any enemies.

In the dead of night, Alexander was the only one awake. He could not bring himself to go to bed after his experience earlier in the day.

Questions echoed in his mind as he attempted to rationalize what had happened. What condition was Emily in? Would she be the same if he brought her back? How would he find her in a sea of the dead? Who, or what, was listening? However, it was Emily's last message that made Alexander's head swirl with confusion. He wondered whether she was the one in his dreams, and if so, he tried to think about why she would be warning him to go. There must be a connection, but he couldn't fathom what it all meant.

The sound of someone tripping over a bucket caught Alexander's attention and woke Dresden from his sleep.

"What was that?" Dresden asked.

"Someone's out there." Alexander looked out the window to observe a child run out of the village. "There's a kid out there. He's leaving the village."

"Simple kid lost his mind," Dresden grunted. "All right, let's go get him."

They both pursued the boy, who had already disappeared into the wilderness. Unwilling to call out to the missing child for fear of attracting unwanted attention, the two tracked the trail to Julia's cabin. Alexander noticed that the once-thriving ecosystem was dying. From the cabin window, a lone candle flickered in a darkness that blinded the senses. An eerie silence was in the air as not even an insect made a peep. The two snuck up to the window to investigate the light and see if the child was there.

The interior of the cabin was dimly lit by a series of candles scattered around the room. A book was open on the table, written in a cryptic language, indicating it was a book of spells. Next to the book, hanging on the candle, was a silver necklace adorned with a red ruby.

Julia entered the room dressed in a plain white tunic, her hair tied up in a bun, and not a single decoration on her person. She read a series of passages from the book to herself before she stripped naked. Alexander and Dresden looked at each other with a look of confusion. When they returned their attention to the scene inside, a naked Julia had put on the ruby necklace and closed the book. She then walked to a back room before closing the door. Dresden noticed there was a window in the back room before the door closed, and he pulled Alexander around the cabin to find it.

"Haven't had enough of a show?" Alexander mocked.

"Like you wouldn't want to," Dresden fired back. "There's something off here."

The two reached the window where they were able to see where Julia went. It was a bedroom, and the boy they'd followed lay on the bed dressed in another plain white tunic.

"What in the...?" Alexander pondered.

Julia leaned over the boy to whisper something into his ear. The boy nodded as she finished speaking to him, and then closed his eyes. From behind the pillow, Julia pulled out a dagger and stabbed the boy in the chest. The boy convulsed and twitched for a brief moment until his body went limp.

Alexander jumped at the sight, but Dresden grabbed him to remain quiet as they watched what happened next. As the boy's body went limp, a ghastly fog arose from it. The aberration lingered in the air for a moment before it was absorbed by the ruby on Julia's necklace. The horror of the scene was not lost on Dresden, who was shocked by what he'd just witnessed.

"It's unfortunate that you had to see this, travelers," Herald said from behind them. Alexander and Dresden turned to find a crowd of villagers.

"Monsters!" Dresden yelled. "How can you do this?"

"Survival, my friend. Surely you can relate to the struggle?" Herald said.

"How can this be about survival? You just murdered one of your own children!"

"I suppose I might be able to shed some light here," Julia announced as she walked up, dressed in the white tunic and necklace. "It *is* about survival, *my survival*, to be exact."

"This is blood magic, the worst of the worst," Alexander said.

"In excess, yes. There was certainly a time where I denounced the taboo as much as the most pious. Nevertheless, Essence is very much a perishable resource to a mage. If you don't find a source to replenish, then the power fades and then disappears," Julia explained.

"So, you kill children to save your own power?" Dresden judged.

"Well, every human is born with Essence within them. It goes away as we grow older, unless you learn how to use it, but children contain the best quality of Essence before it degrades. Since all the other methods of gaining Essence are essentially gone, I need children to regain my strength. If I lose my power, I can't do what I do for these people and the withdrawal I'll go through would likely kill me."

"And you all are okay with this?" Alexander questioned the crowd. "You give up innocent children to this?"

"She needs her energy, it feeds us, it protects us, it surrounds us with the world that you see here." Herald pointed to the surrounding plant life that had sprung back to life. "Our community is blessed to have her. Our lives are easier because of it. We sacrifice a few of our brave young so that the rest can have a chance at a normal future."

"But is it worth giving up your humanity? To give into the darkest parts of magic for the lure of a better life?" Alexander pressed.

"You clearly haven't suffered as we have. You don't know what it means to lose everything and everyone you care about!" Herald yelled.

"I have felt the pain of losing someone!" Alexander fired back.

"How many times?"

"What does it matter how many?"

"I'll tell you why. I had to watch as my six children, one being no more than an infant, were murdered in front of my very eyes! My wife was raped by raving lunatics that called me an enemy because I was born under a different-colored flag! Then I had to watch endless amounts of families suffer the same damn fate!" Herald raged as the crowd nodded in agreement. "All of us here have suffered through the horrors that exist out there. So, do you really believe that you know what it means to suffer like we have?"

Alexander remained silent at the question, unable to find the words to describe the experience and pain that brought him to this world that he did not understand. He wondered how he really could understand how Herald felt. He'd lost his family, while Alexander only lost one person.

"No, you don't. I sure hope that you never have to go through the desperation we have. But if you do, only then will you understand the tough decisions that needed to be made to achieve just a little bit of solace in this life," Herald lectured.

"Blood magic is the darkest, evilest, embodiment of power in the world. You surrender what it means to be human by acquiescing to its lure," Dresden argued after Alexander was left at a loss for words.

"You might be right. We probably did stray from humanity by embracing the darkest of magic. But, from the things I've seen, humanity is capable of actions that are far darker than the most evil and sinister of magic. With that, I am happy to stray as far away as I can," Herald argued.

"Well, I guess there's no point in arguing this further," Dresden concluded. "We might as well leave."

"Indeed, it seems," Herald agreed as he gestured a person to throw Alexander and Dresdan the supplies they'd gathered. "I wish you safe travels, but never return."

"Good luck, Warden, with everything," Julia said.

Alexander said nothing as they gathered their gear and left the village behind, for good.

CHAPTER 8
A FATEFUL RECLAMATION

After a day's worth of travel in random directions to avoid any potential followers from the village, the two decided to encamp for a brief respite. As Alexander slept under the cover of dead leaves, an uncomfortable sensation begun to take hold of his senses. Each breath became harder as the moments went on. Sleep became impossible for him as this sensation began to plague him like a sore that just wouldn't go away. No matter how hard he tried, the feeling only intensified until he was more than uncomfortable. There was a snap inside him that filled him with panic stricken adrenalin that launched him to his feet. Cold sweat beaded across his forehead as he frantically scanned the surrounding area. But, there was nothing but the tall, barren trees cracking in the brisk breeze. Although the lack of sunlight made it nearly impossible to tell the time, judging by the added darkness, it had to be nighttime, and Dresden was nowhere to be found.

"Everything alright?" Dresden asked from his lookout in a nearby tree, "Awful jumpy all of a sudden."

Alexander thought for a moment on how to describe the strange force that came over him. He turned towards where he believed the origin was. "There's something out there, I think. Not sure how to describe it, but whatever it is…it's calling to me."

Dresden jumped down to meet Alexander, "Probably just a bad dream or somethin' about being in a different environment that's causing you to spook."

"No," Alexander dismissed, "Almost like were being watched, being-"

"Stalked, like a predator?" Dresden wondered. A lifetime of experiences made him want to dismiss his companion's worry. Alexander was an outsider that clearly had never experienced a world such as this, and Dresdan wondered if he'd ever experienced the outdoors at all. But this naïve fool was a force that he never met before, a Warden. Legends were full of outlandish claims about their abilities, like being able to fly, having super strength and weapons and armor stronger than anything ever forged, and being able to wield Essence in its purest form. However, he saw nothing in this supposed Warden that would prove these stories, except for the bulletproof shield. But, perhaps there were some aspects about him that were extraordinary, so maybe this supposed disturbance was worth exploring. "Can't hurt to go check out," he said.

"You think so?" Alexander asked, slightly shocked that Dresden appeared to believe him.

"Only for a little bit, if it's East where this force is comin' from, we would be wise to not go too far that way." Dresden rubbed his armored face in thought, "If the rumors I keep hearing from the occasional refugee on the road are true, might be a rather large battle about to commence in that direction."

"It's probably nothing, though," Alexander lied in an effort to ignore the issue in the hopes that it would go away. But as the force strengthened its pull, he failed. Alexander took out his compass. It pointed in a different direction than where this force was pulling him to. Doubt entered his mind about exploring the source. As if the force sensed his hesitancy, the force began to change. He soon felt a calming sensation with a lingering danger. It was calmly calling to him, but threatening him as well if he chose to ignore it. "Nope, yeah, never mind, let's go figure this out."

Dresden nodded in agreement and gestured for Alexander to take the lead. Without hesitation the two started to hunt for the origin of this mysterious force. Alexander found it harder to keep track of where he took his steps. The forest grew more claustrophobic as the trees clustered closer together. At times, the way became so narrow that the men had to turn sideways to continue forward. Although bare of vegetation, the trees soon added another shade of darkness to the already sunless sky.

Alexander noticed something different the farther they went into the forest. Each tree began to bare a marking carved into the bark. Each symbol was odd and did not match any language that either of them knew. Dresden mentioned that they might have been created by superstitious lunatics. The markings were peculiar in their incomplete circular shape with a dot in the gap of the circle. The further they went; the markings were more detailed and turned into hieroglyphs depicting figures from the sky, underground, and earth engaging in combat with one another. There were stories of figures that fought with swords, guns, strange machines against monsters and other such things.

The forest ended abruptly in an open clearing with strange structures. Ancient in their appearance, the buildings were magnificent in their scale. Columns, arches, causeways, temples, and other structures were everywhere. Time had taken their toll on the buildings, but they were still a remarkable sight to the travelers.

"What... is this place?" Alexander marveled.

"Ruins of some kind."

"Out in the middle of nowhere? No roads, no signs? Strange. Almost looks like it was abandoned for no reason."

"There's always a reason. Must have been abandoned some time ago, and I'm talking a long time ago," Dresden observed.

"Might as well look around, see if there's anything of value," Alexander suggested.

"That's using the old noggin, at least you're learning."

The two split up and explored separate parts of the area. The buildings were even more magnificent inside. Alexander entered a building surrounded by elegant and towering columns. A massive room filled with lines of columns created a path to a large statue. The statue itself depicted a heroic man on a throne. The man was dressed and configured to appear as a God. This place must have been some kind of house of worship. The statue's face was bearded and strong featured. Alexander could have pondered for hours as to the details behind the statue and the society itself, but with no knowledge of any of the writings or symbols inscribed inside the building, there was little reason to investigate. He was there searching for supplies, after all.

Such a strange place. Like a tomb.

As Alexander turned to leave, a glow emanated from behind the statue. He investigated its origin to find it was coming from a pedestal atop a platform in the center of the room. The room itself seemed to form around the pedestal as the columns encircled the area. The mysterious glow was a mixture of red and orange, with flakes of black orbiting in the center. Cautiously, he moved closer to the hypnotizing glow. It began to flicker the closer he got. The black flakes danced frantically as Alexander raised his hand to the glow. It began to form into an orb that was ready to receive his touch. Once he touched it, a blinding light shot forth and knocked him to the ground with a tremendous force.

Alexander slowly got up, his hand burning. He examined it but found nothing unusual. However, a crowd of ghostly figures surrounded him in a prostrated stance. Silent and still. Alexander cautiously attempted to step away from the area, but found himself surrounded by the crowd of silent phantoms that prostrated themselves on the ground.

A loud yell from behind jolted Alexander as he saw a tall ghost dressed in elaborate red clothing gesture and address the room, ignoring Alexander as if he was not even there. The voice was muffled and inaudible, but the emotion behind the orator was powerful. A command was given that made the crowd raise their heads from the ground. One of them was helped up from the ground by the leader and appeared to be consoled. The leader turned back toward the center and uttered a rhythmic chant that was joined by the rest of the crowd in unison.

The chant grew louder as a red aura emanated from the crowd that formed – it was the red glow Alexander initially saw. As the glow grew brighter to the point of being blinding, the ghosts disappeared in a flash.

A haunting silence lingered in the building as Alexander looked around in bewilderment. Without hesitation, he ran out of the building, tightly holding the hand that had touched the unknown glow. Alexander eventually reunited with Dresden at the center of the settlement.

"Anything?" Alexander asked.

"Nah, nothing. From the looks of it, this place hasn't been lived in for a long time. Not even nomads. You find anything?"

Alexander paused before answering. He wanted to tell him about what happened, but the urge was suppressed by the realization that he still did not understand what he had experienced. The last thing he wanted to do was potentially scare away his only companion. Maybe it was nothing, he thought to himself. "Didn't find anything either. Maybe whoever carved those markings in the trees squatted here for a time."

"Doubt they lived here. Probably got spooked by the place and marked it as a no go zone." Dresden looked around. "As good a place as ever to stay and rest for a little."

The travelers set up a place to rest in one of the nearby structures that provided protection from anything that might come. A few hours passed before Alexander was awoken by the roar of thunder that repeated itself in an unusual rhythm. Dresden was nowhere to be found in the immediate area, much to Alexander's surprise.

Where in the— The bastard left me!

He proceeded outside to look around, only to be met by another thunderous roar. The horizon was lit by a red glow that pierced the clouds. Crashes and grinding echoed after the thunder. Rather than searching the surrounding structures, he decided to investigate the phenomenon.

Outside of town, Alexander traversed a hill, intent on finding what caused the glow. The terrain was a mud-filled mess further complicated by a recent rainfall. Alexander finally reached the top of the hill.

In the distance, a sea of men charged at each other in successive order under a rain of fire that flew across the sky. Strange machines rolled across the surface, spewing death on anything that lay in front of them. For every crack of thunder, the ground exploded with such force that soil, along with anything on it, was thrown weightlessly into the air.

"Thought you might come here," Dresden said as he revealed himself, "Quite a view, ain't it?"

"Spectacular. Horrifyingly spectacular." Alexander struggled to find words to fit the situation, "Why?'

"Not a clue anymore. Politics was never my interest."

"How long do these battles go on?"

"Depends. Usually they average about a month or so. Everyone thinks they can overpower the other, I guess."

"That long... such madness." Alexander was struck by the amount of destruction being wrought by each side.

"Might look like madness from up here, but down there with all the heat and metal, people being obliterated around you with no place to go but forward into the meat grinder, it is worse than death," Dresden said as he observed the battle. "They'll drop enough rounds on that area to make it nothing but glass. By the end of it... nothing will be left."

"I never knew such power was being wielded down here."

"You all don't know much, do you?" Dresden wondered before looking around at their surroundings, "We should keep moving."

"Back to the town?"

"No, farther along. These battles tend to scatter anyone or anything in the surrounding area. We'd be better off if we stay ahead of them."

Alexander took a last glance at the battle raging in the distance. The inferno appeared to intensify as Dresden led him away.

"The one good thing about a battle is that there must be a settlement nearby," Dresden mentioned.

"How do you know that?"

"Most armies tend to name their battles after the nearest settlements for their records. Let's just hope they aren't fighting over ruins."

After a few hours of travel the two had put some distance between them and the battle. As they began descending down a hill, Dresden stopped all of a sudden. Snapping branches alerted them that something was coming. Dresden looked around to try to find the source, but the sounds seemed to come from all around them. He rushed to find some cover, but decided that nothing out in the open was safe. A group of downed trees caught Dresden's attention, and he gestured Alexander to come take cover quickly. Figures began to appear over the hill behind them.

They both crawled slowly under a fallen tree and stayed still. The stale silence was broken by the sound of footsteps around them. Alexander carefully looked to his side to see a pair of feet clothed in poor looking sandals that likely provided more discomfort than bare feet. Many more crowded around the individual and walked around the area speaking a strange language in an increasingly aggressive tone.

Out of curiosity, Alexander positioned himself so he could peek out and see who the people were. Ragged and dirty men and women rushed about. Each one of them was armed with whatever could be used as a weapon. In their native tongue, they yelled at one another with gestures that symbolized blame. One of the men, in a fit, threw down his spear in front of one of the others, which caused another to punch him. A brawl between the two broke out and they wrestled each other to the ground. Alexander flinched, as the fighters were low enough to see under the tree. Dresden frantically signaled for him to crawl back farther, to no avail. Alexander was frozen in fear.

Then silence fell. The men on the ground stopped fighting and got up. The others stopped talking. Alexander's ears began to ring just as everyone turned to look in the opposite direction. Out of the woods appeared a figure dressed in black robes, its face covered by the shroud of its hood. It addressed them.

Alexander could not hear the conversation as the ringing in his ears increased to a chilling pitch. A freezing cold spread from the tip of his appendages throughout his body. Dresden pulled him under the tree and found that Alexander was suffering from a sort of paralysis. A white haze covered his terror-stricken eyes. Dresden muffled Alexander before the others could hear him cry out. Alexander slipped into unconsciousness.

Alexander woke in a fright to find himself still in the wilderness, but in a ditch warmed by a fire. Dresden sat at other end of the fire, cleaning his hidden blades.

"Passed out again, but luckily only for a few hours," Dresden sighed.

"I don't know what happened. I was looking at the people who were by us and then…"

"Then?"

"Something, or someone, came. Dressed in all black robes, moving like a ghost. The people changed when it came. One moment, they were acting like animals and then they became… possessed."

"Well, I'll tell you this, you were the one who looked possessed when I pulled you back under the tree." Dresden gave Alexander a cup of soup made from some of the supplies the villagers packed for them the previous day.

"Didn't you see it?"

"No, I was doing the intelligent thing and stayed hidden. I didn't catch a glimpse of your *phantom*," Dresden remarked, unconvinced.

"What? You don't believe I saw something?"

"Of all the years I've spent in my travels, I have yet to encounter some dark phantom wandering about. I'm pretty sure if there were any mythical ghosts out there, they wouldn't really be interested in dealing with simple barbarians," Dresden explained.

"I know what I saw," Alexander objected.

"In any case, I got to see something interesting while you were out," Dresden countered. "Farther along the route we were heading is an encampment of some kind."

"Really? How many?"

"Not sure."

"Think they're friendly?"

Dresden adjusted his blades as he reequipped them and sighed. "Well, we're going to find out."

"Why? I thought you wanted to avoid all contact?"

"Well, I didn't necessarily get away quietly." Dresden stood and put his hands on his hips.

Nearly a dozen individuals appeared out of the woods and surrounded Dresden and Alexander. They were armed with a variety of weapons and dressed in ragged purple clothing peppered with ill-fitting metal armor. Dresden gestured with his hands that he was not a threat, while Alexander jumped to his feet. His instinct was to grab his weapon, but he was waved off by Dresden.

"Relax; they're not going to kill us."

"How would you know that?"

"Because, we'd already be dead."

Chapter 9
Shadows of Intent

Under heavy guard, Alexander and Dresden were escorted back to their captors' encampment. The camp was more like a town, littered with hastily built dwellings designed with a sort of architectural elegance. Arches, buttresses, domes, and decorated columns peppered the area. The ambitious designs were built by a diverse amount of scavenged materials and covered with cloaks that gave the tents a colorful appearance. Colored flags were strung from building to building; mysterious symbols were painted in lavish colors on the walls and columns to give a festive atmosphere that signaled the settlement was preparing for an upcoming event.

One of the most common devices Alexander could see were carts, so many carts. They came in all shapes and sizes, next to every building and used by practically everyone. The guards were dressed in armor that fit their lifestyle, mobile, only covering the most sensitive areas of the body. The rest was covered with either simple cloth or leather. Each of them had symbols painted on their faces of different colors and in different styles.

The people of the camp came out to witness the strangers who were brought to their home. Alexander looked at the crowds that gathered around and saw the same kind of faces as they'd seen in the previous settlement. These people all wore togas over layers of other mismatched clothing. As they were led to the center of the settlement, it changed from tents into multi-storied buildings that served various purposes such as dwellings and markets. The center of the town was an open area that housed a stone temple of simple design. Its simplistic architecture and lack of decoration made it a unique structure in the lavishly decorated settlement.

Alexander and Dresden were led into the temple where they passed a number of simply dressed priests until they reached the main room of the building. Inside, there was a lone altar made of stone covered in carved symbols.

Alexander recalled the mysterious temple where he encountered the ghosts. However, the symbols were different and appeared even more ancient in their nature. The rest of the room was covered in a plethora of banners, parchments, paintings and other visuals such as ancient writings in various languages and hieroglyphs that displayed many different scenes in mythology which painted a narrative of an epic history. Alexander and Dresden were pushed in front of an altar and forced to their knees.

"Oh, the Gods, they're going to sacrifice us!" Alexander yelled to Dresden.

"Relax."

"How are you this calm?"

"Because," an old man said, coming out of the shadows, "the man knows that organized human sacrifice died out long ago. Why waste meat to those who left us, when we could use it?" The man raised his hands out of his long sleeves, "Not that we use human meat. We're certainly no barbarians."

The old man's extravagant clothing was more flamboyant than the rest.

"Come now, you can stand on your feet." The man gestured to them before turning his attention to the guards. "Leave us."

"Who are you?" Alexander asked.

"I? Oh, I'm just a simple man. A man with memories, none of which are my own. I know who you are though."

Alexander turned to Dresden. "I guess you're not as stealthy as you would have me believe."

Dresden let out a grunt at the notion. "Listen, I was only looking ahead on the trail. We meant to avoid you, no harm intended."

"Not you, my iron friend. You," the man said, turning to Alexander. "I've seen you... in my dreams, Warden."

"Odd," Dresden commented.

Alexander balked at the revelation. "What?"

"I sensed your presence when you came to this world, Warden. The whispers within my dreams spoke of the return." The man scratched his white beard with intrigue. "And it seems you have changed things."

"I haven't done anything here," Alexander declared.

"Your weapons, your compass. They are filled with the purest Essence," the man said to Alexander's surprise, since his weapons and other things were still hidden beneath his cloak.

"You can sense the Essence?" Alexander questioned.

"Indeed. I was taught to sense the power by my master long ago, as did his master to him, and so on and so forth."

"Can you wield it?"

"No, no normal man can ever wield it, only sense it if they're trained to."

Dresden groaned, "Oh, don't tell me that you two are talking about that magical nonsense."

"Not much of a believer in the power of the Essence?" the old man asked.

"Doesn't really matter, does it? Believe? Even if I did, it doesn't make it alive here in this dead world. Essence died here along with the myths," Dresden explained.

"Belief is a powerful thing; it can create and destroy. It can also drive us to take great leaps into the unknown. Am I correct in assuming so, Alexander?"

"You know my name?" Alexander asked in awe. He hadn't introduced himself.

"A name that can bring greatness back to this decrepit world," the old man said.

"All right, you already know his name and have graced us with all these cryptic words. Now, how about you tell us who you are and why you brought us here?" Dresden demanded.

"But of course. I have many names, my friend—The Keeper, High Priest, The Librarian, The Giver, The Protector of Our Heritage, and so on. However, since you are not of my people, you can call me by my earliest name, Gannon. As for your presence here, when I first sensed that a Warden had appeared, I had to try to bring you here if I could. I have no favor to ask of you, I just wanted to see if the visions I had were more than the visions of an old man with a withering mind," Gannon explained.

"Subtlety altruistic, or at least as close as it gets to it in this world," Dresden commented.

"And your pessimism lacks the subtlety you claim I have. Your past must be wrought with tragedies that turned promise into pessimism,"

Gannon observed. "Alas, your past is yours and yours alone. The future, however, belongs to both of you together. Alexander, I am sure the purpose of your journey here is noble."

Alexander looked to Dresden with a worried gaze, then sighed.

"You're here to find one of your own, another Warden?" Dresden suggested.

"Yes, another Warden, but not to find," Gannon surmised.

"Retrieve," Alexander said. "I'm here to retrieve a Warden who is very special to me. She was taken, tragically and unjustly."

"Tragically?" Dresden muttered to himself.

"A tale as old as time, man seeking woman. Are you responsible for her disappearance? The grief I can feel from your voice makes you sound responsible," Gannon suggested.

"No!" Alexander blasted. "She was taken!"

"To where?" Gannon asked.

Alexander slouched and took a deep breath. "To The Abyss."

CHAPTER 10
ABYSMAL MOTIVES

The Abyss. Upon hearing this, Dresden swirled into a rage that prompted the guards to return for precaution. Gannon attempted to calm him down, but to no avail. He had reason to be upset about the revelation, not many people would want to hear that they were on a journey to the underworld.

Through the entire history of written civilization, there was always the belief in an underworld within the major belief systems. Even at the most fractious times of faith, this belief remained constant. The Abyss itself was said to be ruled by a single deity that had no name, since it was thought that death was a realm where worldly names were not necessary. Other than in legends, no one was ever said to cross into The Abyss as a living person. There have been cults, usually led by mages, that revered the land of the dead and tried to cross into it by manipulating Essence, the mysterious force that pervades the world. Those who practiced this pursuit were usually the target of purges, because many considered their efforts Black Magic.

This history was not lost on Dresden and, coupled with his lack of belief, added to his shock when he heard the true nature of Alexander's motivation.

"The Abyss!" Dresden raged. "This woman of yours is dead? This isn't a retrieval; this is a damn resurrection!"

"Indeed, a most incredible task," Gannon commented.

"Incredible?" Dresden balked. "This is the most idiotic and asinine idea I have ever heard."

"My journey—" Alexander attempted to explain.

"Your journey is about resurrecting a soul from the land of the dead! Look around, this whole world is the land of the dead. The countless lives I have seen taken to the underworld for no reason, all the lives you saw end without reason... What makes this person so worth bringing back? How is it even possible that someone can have this... mindset?" Dresden threw up his arms in anger, "What the hell can a single woman be to cause a dimwit like you to throw your life away like this? You must be a special kind of imbecile!"

"Oh, I'm the imbecile?" Alexander shot back as he rose to his feet.

"Yeah you are! Are you what makes her so special, huh? A good piece of ass? Prettiest girl that ever talked to you? Some other hormonal reason?"

"No, no that's not the reason."

"Well then, what is it? Because you can't get over how shit happens and life takes more than gives?"

Alexander finally had enough. His face was red with anger and he couldn't hold back any longer. "Because she saved me!" he exploded.

Dresden huffed at the response and stormed out without saying a word.

"Let him go," Gannon said to Alexander, who motioned as if to stop him from trying to bring Dresden back. "I guess you didn't inform your partner about the true nature of your quest."

"I left out certain aspects of it," Alexander admitted as his anger dissipated and a feeling of sorrow overcame him. "He is right, though."

Gannon sat down in one of the chairs he'd had a guard bring in earlier, then gestured for Alexander to sit as he gathered his thoughts.

"Never did I think this place would be like it is," Alexander said. "My focus and path was clear as day before I arrived, but... this place has no day, and I simply cannot fathom any of it. The grief I have suffered with for so long has been dwarfed... in an instant. There was a boy, when I first arrived, he was so young, and this world has people in it who were so heartless as to kill him in cold blood. What is my grief, compared to that of the mother who had to watch her son die?"

"This world is cruel to all things, I'm afraid. Do you feel bad about what you're doing?" Gannon asked.

"I'm... ashamed. Who am I to know what it means to lose someone and feel depression when this is the way of the world? The stories have always said that we were the ones who protected all, but we failed. Here I stand before you, a Warden, burdened with great purpose... with the selfish goal of saving the one I love."

"The stories and old writings say much about your people and their purposes. None of that matters though, Alexander. This is your story."

"But is it worth writing?" Alexander's eyes moistened with tears. "Everything in my heart says that it is worth the pain and difficulty, but it wasn't supposed to be like this... none of this. I look at what is around me and ask if this world needs this story of mine? My heart, my very soul, is becoming twisted by this darkness that I've seen, that I feel is out there waiting."

Gannon rose from his chair and with his finger, traced the outline of the worn-out inscriptions on the altar. "I have seen all sorts of motivations drive men in this world. Fear has always been the driving force behind all our actions down here. Fear of the unknown, fear of starvation, fear of losing power, fear of just about anything. These are the only stories I have seen in my time. Long gone are the quests for others, peace, and the jewels of our mythical world," Gannon said, finishing his inspection of the inscriptions. "Alexander, this is your story. If it is something you feel deeply about, then go and accomplish it. A quest for love is something that may not be what others would expect or want of someone like you, but a journey like that is exactly what this world could use."

"What about Dresden?"

"Your friend? Oh, I wouldn't worry about him. He clearly thought you had a different motive behind your journey. Let him go cool off before you try to approach him. Other than that, I welcome you to stay the evening. Fortunately, today is a special day for our people; we're celebrating our ancestors with our most sacred relic."

"I would be honored to be part of your ceremony and thank you for your hospitality."

Gannon called a guard in and instructed him to escort Alexander to a tent to rest, then he turned to another man at his side.

"Double the guard," Gannon said. "I sense a disturbance."

CHAPTER 11
AN ENDLESS LEGEND

The people of the camp brought in twigs, sticks, and logs to the front of the temple. A few men worked to build a structure meant to hold something. Dresden sat around one of the surrounding fires with a blank stare as he sculpted a stick into a small blade. Thunder roared across the sky as the work continued without a flinch from the laborers. The air was thick with the musk of fresh-killed game and the entrails left for the dogs. The community was destitute and poor at its core, with noticeable signs that it was one step away from collapse. However, these people were different in Dresden's view. Despite their desperation, these people had a quiet dignity in their behavior. Even the most mundane of tasks were done with precision and pride.

"You know what it means to barely cling to your own sense of humanity," a hooded Gannon commented as he sat down next to Dresden.

"Make a lot of assumptions, old man. Might be able to read the Warden, but I wouldn't advise you cling to the false belief that you can figure me out."

"And I'd advise you to not cling to the façade that you claim is your personality," Gannon accused with a grin. The accusation prompted a visibly annoyed Dresden to stop carving and sigh heavily. "Style yourself a loner?" Gannon continued. "Just wandering about the world for yourself, I would assume by the way that you act. No. There's something deeper within your heart."

"Digging in the wrong spot."

"Oh, come on now. A loner wouldn't travel with some random person. Turned out to be a Warden, yes, but you didn't know that at first. When you first saw him, you must have thought he was just some freak running around with a sword, not knowing which end was up."

"He and a kid were about to get killed."

"Let me guess; you did it for the kid?" Gannon suggested to a nodding Dresden. "Regardless, you kept him around afterward."

"Your point, what is it!"

"You are a man who lives for purpose. I don't know what you did in your past, but I know it was something with meaning and you want that again. Explains why you were so upset with Alexander's admission."

"It's a joke."

"His motivation?"

"The whole damn thing. Wardens are meant to be more than a hormonal kid wanting his dead girlfriend back," Dresden huffed as he went back to carving.

"No bigger grief than losing someone you love. It can drive a person to do..." Gannon stopped and gazed out in a blank stare.

"All right there?"

"Hm? Yes, quite all right. I think you might not fully understand the true power behind Alexander's motivations. Perhaps you don't know what it means to lose someone," Gannon said to Dresden, which prompted him to stop carving once again.

"I know loss; I know what it means to lose."

"Haven't we all?"

"All right!" Dresden cried, annoyed enough to raise his voice for a moment before he calmed down. "What am I missing with Alexander's little quest?"

"How familiar are you with the Endless Legends?"

Dresden silently shook his head. Gannon went on to explain that there have always been legends and myths throughout history. Many of them vary by culture or race and were forgotten after those sources were extinguished. However, a line of legends has existed since the beginning of time, created by the first known race called the Builders. Their legends were known as the Endless Legends, due to their inability to be extinguished.

Along with their longevity, the Endless Legends were known to describe key moments that altered or reset the order of the world. The Endless Legends were usually interpreted as prophecies that told of future events along with events of the past. Other interpretations were that the Legends were self-fulfilling prophecies that could inspire a person to achieve a goal greater than any other if they were inspired enough.

Many cults throughout time were solely devoted to fulfilling the Endless Legends to achieve higher levels of consciousness. The fear of individuals being motivated to change the order of nature for their own gain led many kings and races to bury the existence of the Endless Legends. Much of the knowledge about them was eradicated from public knowledge and confined to guarded libraries. A series of wars led to the destruction of the libraries that held the Legends, so they were considered lost. Few remain who actually knew a specific Legend within the series, and those who knew them did not speak of them out of fear.

"All right so there's a series of stories—"

"Prophecies," Gannon corrected.

"People have died over them. What does this have to do with me? Or Alex?"

"My position has been passed down for centuries. I carry the entire history of our people. Along with our history—"

"You know the legends," Dresden concluded.

"Indeed, I do, only one," Gannon admitted as he pulled out a piece of parchment. The markings on it looked like someone copied it from a rock using the broadside of chalk. Dresden took the parchment and glanced at it.

"You are holding perhaps one of the most valuable items in the world right now," Gannon told him.

"A piece of paper? With lettering I can't even decipher? Quite valuable," Dresden said with a hint of sarcasm.

"Well, not everything of value is gold or jewels. This was etched by some unknown soul who had the foresight to copy that inscription down before the source was destroyed forever from the ravages of time."

"So, a very old piece. Just carry this stuff around in your pocket like spare change?" Dresden wondered.

"Well, no," Gannon admitted as he took back the item. "Would probably get in a bit of trouble if others knew I was being so hazardous, but that's neither here or there."

"So, what does it say?"

"Interpreting dead languages is always a tough thing. That's why I can only tell you what was told to me that was told to the person before and so on." He cleared his throat. *"From the depths of death, one will be risen to light the world."*

"A riddle. Why does everything have to be a riddle?"

"It certainly was a riddle to me, until you and Alexander came here."

"So, you think his quest to revive his girlfriend is what those folks predicted all the way back to creation? The seminal moment where the order of nature will be reset?

"I'm not so sure about the reset of nature, but I do believe the success of Alexander would bring back the light that has gone from this world."

"You mean the sun?"

"I mean love."

"Well, now we're going a little off the trail here."

"No! I assure you we are right within the bounds of sanity. Can you not feel the cold? The emptiness? The loneliness that prevails across this world? We, as a people, have lost our connection to this world, the Gods, and each other."

"And all we need is love?" Dresden mocked.

"Have you ever thought that love was cold? Empty? Or lonely? Listen to me, Dresden; I'm not speaking about this in some kind of romantic fairy tale sense. This is about the restoration of the part of our species that makes us different from the animals. Alexander being able to snatch a soul away from the cold darkness of The Abyss would upset the whole order of existence. Things would change. I'm not sure what, but the way the world is now will not be the same."

"I agree that being able to raise the dead would certainly be a bit of a game changer. But the fantastical—"

"Ask yourself this, why did you keep Alexander around after your first encounter?"

"I thought he would be able to help."

"You certainly didn't think he would just slay his way to a better world?"

"Not really. He doesn't seem like the 'slaying' type."

"You knew he was meant to serve a purpose, a purpose you might not relate to, but a purpose nonetheless."

"Perhaps."

CHAPTER 12
REKINDLING

*T*he sun had gone dim, and the sky went dark. The once colorful life had become gray with a staleness that reflected a slow excruciating decay. Against a tree, a tired, dirty, and scuffed Alexander leaned to gather his thoughts. His shivers forced his visible breath to stutter out onto the frail tree bark. Once again, he heard the woman in the distance. However, there were no hums, only his name being uttered in a repetitive and hypnotic rhythm. As he walked to where the woman last was, the statues of heroes were cracked, broken, and mangled. The cobblestone path was now dirty and covered by a layer of dead leaves. The woman was still standing at the edge in the same pristine white dress.

Against his better judgement, he continued toward her as she called to him. Something caught his step and tripped him. As he fell to the ground her calls stopped.

Alexander woke to the sight of a skull close to him. He jolted back, only to find that he was surrounded by a seemingly endless sea of bones. In his terror he looked toward the woman who still faced away. She was accompanied by a dark, phantom-like figure that seemed to stare right at him. Above them swirled a blood-red vortex in the sky. His body froze despite his efforts to move, as the gaze of the figure hardened. Alexander's *chest grew heavy, his breaths more labored and a burning sensation spread from his hand to the rest of his body. Screams were pointless, as the noise never escaped his mouth. The burning continued. It escalated. There was nothing to hear except the words of the woman who calmly uttered, "You should have stayed."*

***

Alexander jolted awake; his eyes scanned the room around him for any intruders. There was no one, only a light that projected through the opening of the tent. A cold sweat beaded off his tired face as he got up to find the source. Outside, the darkness was lit from a sizable bonfire that towered in the air high above any of the surrounding structures. The fire was surrounded on all sides by the townsfolk, and Dresden was alone closest to the flames. He walked down to the fire and went to Dresden, who just finished carving a stick to mere splinters. Alexander sat down and immediately felt the intense heat.

"I'm not sure whether you're crazy or will just go to incredible lengths to be alone," Alexander joked.

"What do you mean?" Dresden responded with little interest.

"There isn't anyone within a few dozen feet of you."

"Maybe I'm not that interesting."

"Or probably due more to the ungodly heat you feel so interested in subjecting yourself to."

"Could be."

"Could be?" Alexander said as he wordlessly gestured to the lack of people around.

"When you've wandered the wilderness as long as I have," Dresden said, "you know a luxury when you see it. This fire gives the kind of heat that I haven't felt in a very long time," he explained, pointing to the forest outside of camp.

The two sat for a while in silence as the fired roared on. Alexander gestured as if he wanted to say something, but was unable to get anything out. All he could think about was mending what happened earlier and perhaps even apologizing. Dresden was no fool; he knew something was on Alexander's mind. However, Dresden had a few questions of his own.

"You said earlier this woman saved you, how is that?" Dresden asked, to Alexander's surprise.

Alexander tripped over his words as he tried to respond before he was ready, "Yeah, yes, yes she did."

"Just calm yourself down and tell me what she did that was so important that you literally jumped from the top of the world to come down here."

"Well, I mean, it's a lot to cover."

"I have time."

"See, my parents died when I was very young, twelve years old really. I didn't really have anyone family wise, they all died or I just didn't ever know them. Grew up under the care of priests and monks in the Temple of the Goddess'. They loved those goddess' more than me, that's for sure. By the time I turned sixteen I had enough of the neglect, punishment, and abuse all in the name of learning to respect and sacrifice for the divine. Those were some crazy monks. But, instead of running away, because there are only so many places to go, I walked out to the edge of the land, intent on jumping."

"Isn't that what you did to come down here?" Dresden questioned.

"Well yes, with one small caveat. The monks had a few remaining elixirs that give temporary invulnerability to immense trauma, not much else though."

"Impressive. Sounds like a substance they wouldn't just give away," Dresden said.

"Oh absolutely not. It's beyond a crime to possess it. Even worse, to use it to go to the forbidden…this world that is."

Dresden chuckled at the label. "Forbidden? Ironic name, whatever was the reason for you all packing up and leaving?"

"I'm afraid I'm without answers to that one. Not that I haven't tried to find an answer cooped up with all those books. There just weren't any."

"So you were on the verge of killing yourself?"

"Oh yeah." Alexander's posture slumped as he remembered. "It seemed like the only thing to do, food had lost its taste, the wind its coolness, the sun no longer warmed me, jokes didn't make me laugh. I had friends, but the only thing I could feel was loneliness…that is until she called out to me. Emily."

"Emily is her name?" Dresden suggested to a nodding Alexander.

"Only knew her for a few days, met through a friend. Would never have guessed she remembered my name. The most gorgeous girl I had ever seen, and with a voice that just pierced through the layers of darkness in my mind that had been building up for years. And the funny thing is, she wasn't even panicky or anything like you would think someone would react in that situation." Alexander chuckled as he analyzed his own story.

"How did this person react?"

"Calmly. Just put her arm around me and said, 'You should stay.' After that we became close friends, inseparable."

"Guess the romance sparked up along the way naturally," Dresden concluded as he stared at the raging fire.

"Well, my romance started, yeah."

"Hm? We're you two even a thing?"

"I wanted to be, but-"

Dresden put his face in his hands and started shaking his head. "Oh no, no, no, no. You got to be kidding me. Please tell me that you at least slept together."

Alexander sat there quietly as Dresden slowly turned his gaze on him expecting an answer, but was only met with a blank stare.

"Well-"

"For the love of the Gods, man!"

"Not for lack of trying, I assure you."

Dresden held his own head in disbelief at the revelation that Alexander's lost love wasn't even his actual lover. "So let me get this straight," he grunted, "This girl we're going to save wasn't your girlfriend, wasn't a lover, wasn't even a one night romp. Why in all that is holy would you do all this for her? Tragic that she passed, but Alex, you're not doing all of this under the impression that she'll finally come around to loving you? Please lords, tell me no."

"Thought never entered my mind."

"So why?" Dresden questioned.

"Because it's my fault that she's dead," Alexander admitted in a crackled voice. The pain that the answer brought on him was not lost on Dresden who wore an inquisitive expression.

"Accident?" Dresden probed in a cautious tone.

"No," Alexander let out a deep sigh. "You know how I said that I tried to become more than just friends? Well, it was the third time

I tried that I decided it was time to move on. However, the only way to do that, in my mind at least, was to just cut it off. The talking, the friendship, all that. So I did, made a big fuss, offended her, and burned down every bridge I had with her so that she'd never want to talk to me again. And it worked, I felt better, over it really."

"So what happened next?"

"Unfortunately for her, life didn't get much better. Fell into some hard times and sunk into a dark sea of depression."

"You think that was from what you did?"

"Nah, there's no way I'd self-inflate and think I was so important in her life that she got depressed. Ironically, her depression was more a product of her kindness. She always wanted to help people, even those who couldn't be saved or fixed. Came to a point where she was so focused on helping others, that she took any failure personally, and I guess it took a toll. She tried to help everyone but never gave a thought to helping herself. Her parents found her with her wrists slit one morning, slumped against a statue of our first ancestors, and like that she was gone," Alexander said with almost no emotion. For him, there was only numbness associated with the recollection as the pain was so much it just took away his ability to fully express how much sorrow it made him feel.

"She fell into a depression. You yourself said that it probably wasn't because of you. Shit like that happens," Dresden tried to explain to a reluctant Alexander.

"I know she didn't do it because of me, but I could have helped her. Same as she did for me. She barely even knew me and yet she put herself out there to keep me from ending my own life. And how did I repay her?" Alexander asked, seemingly to himself. "With selfishness, that's what! I couldn't see past my own damn wants. I betrayed her trust. So instead of being there for her in her darkest hour, she was there alone. I could have- "

"Even if you were there," Dresden interjected, "there's no guarantee that you could have saved her."

"Guess I'll never know that. But what I do know is that the old books mentioned a way to The Abyss and that there was a chance to bring a soul back. I know it's an extreme solution, downright lunacy in terms of feasibility, but dammit, this compass I stole guides a person to their destiny and I feel saving her is mine, so I'm going to try! With or without you!" Alexander exploded, to Dresden's surprise.

"Whoa, whoa there," Dresden tried to calm him. "No need to get all defensive. Don't worry, I'll be sticking with you on this one."

"Why would you even care, though?" Alexander questioned with a newly acquired suspicion. "Why did you save me on the road, lead me to that town and stay with me all this way?"

"Because it's my job, it's my duty. A Green Blade never stops protecting a traveler until they arrive at their destination." Dresden saw that Alexander was about to ask the obvious question so he preempted him. "Green Blades were an Order that was around since the beginning, since the first settlements really. Job was simple, we protected traders, pilgrims, pretty much any travelers from bandits, monsters, abusive mages, or whatever else threatened the people. Was part of it all my life until the Order was disbanded, forcefully."

"What caused it to be disbanded?" Alexander inquired.

Dresden battled his own thoughts when searching for an answer. "No," he shook his head, "No, not ready to tell that story. Not yet."

"I just poured out my entire life just a few moments ago," Alexander prodded.

"Well," Dresden shrugged, "we're all different."

"Oh."

"But like I said, I'm with you until the end of your travels. It's all I have left," Dresden assured him.

"Good to know. Thank you."

"Don't mention it."

They both sat quietly in front of the fire and observed the ceremony. Alexander shrugged as he sized up the size of the pyre.

"Why did they build such a big fire? Seems a little unnecessary."

"That priest, Gannon, told me that this was a special day for them. Something about how this is the day when their culture goes through their annual test of worth."

"Curious. So they build a fire?"

"That's a part of it. Look there." Dresden pointed to the temple off to their side as Gannon appeared from it with a posse of plainly dressed priests carrying a large chest by poles on the four corners. The priests carried a thick black stoned chest by resting the poles on their shoulders. The chest's heft showed by the way the priests had to shuffle forward to keep their balance. The chest itself was undecorated, jagged, and black as the night. Inscriptions of different kinds randomly peppered the outside of the chest.

"Apparently, the people here hold their most cherished possessions inside that chest that seems about to crush those malnourished holy men there."

"They aren't malnourished, just naturally smaller in stature," a voice behind them said.

They turned around to see a woman standing behind them, dressed in elaborate-looking armor. She had long brown hair tied up into a ponytail. Her face was worn, but young in appearance and highlighted by a series of cyan-colored markings. The markings showed signs of wear, too, but they were overshadowed by the depth of her almond eyes and dark skin.

"The weakest among us physically are chosen to be the conduits to the divine, while the rest of us are graced with being warriors."

"And who might you be?" Alexander asked.

"My name is Mira, Holy Warden." Mira prostrated before the two of them.

Dresden and Alexander looked to each other in amusement.

"Uh," Alexander stuttered. "Please, I'm not holy. Please, get up, Mira."

"Yeah, if you saw this guy faint at the sound of a few twigs cracking you'd never mistake him for a God," Dresden said. Alexander was not amused.

"How dare you!" Mira yelled as she jumped up. Her hand instantly reached to her sword while Dresden drew his hidden blades.

"Hold up!" Alexander said, stepping between the two before they could lunge at one another.

"You insult the Holy one?" Mira demanded.

"Holy?" Dresden asked.

"Yeah, you keep using that word," Alexander added.

"What do you mean? You are the Warden who was brought in by our scouting party earlier, are you not?"

"Well, yes, that is me," Alexander admitted.

"Then that means you are of the divine's offspring in our eyes."

"That would explain why I just took over someone's tent without anyone caring earlier," Alexander mused.

"Yes, my people revere your race. The protectors who watch over us as you fly through the sky."

"Haven't done the whole flying thing, more familiar with the opposite part... falling," Alexander admitted as everyone calmed down and their weapons were put away.

"The stories might be a little diluted," Mira accepted. "But that doesn't mean this one can insult someone of such stature like you were some kind of commoner."

"I can," Dresden bluntly said.

"Don't put me on a pedestal. I can take some... *constructive* criticisms," Alexander said while he glared at Dresden briefly.

"In any event, I joke with his holiness and he pokes at me for my sins," Dresden sarcastically said.

Mira scoffed at the remark. "Well, I guess that'll have to do. I'm all out of fight for the day anyway." Mira joined them in front of the fire. Before sitting, she drew her sword, which caught the eyes of both men. Mira planted her sword in the ground before taking a seat.

"Much better, could never sit comfortably with that thing," Mira sighed to the men, who stared silently at the sword.

"Tad bigger than mine," Alexander said under his breath.

"Size isn't important," Dresden quipped.

"Said the guy with the butter knives up his wrists."

"I'll remember that, kid."

Mira coughed to get their attention as she noticed them starting at her equipment. "You know, it helps to know how to use it."

The two straightened their backs, coughing, and looking around to gloss over the slightly embarrassing situation.

"I take it you know something about this ceremony that's going on?" Dresden inquired.

"Indeed I do, it's called the Rekindling. When the times call for it, there must be a test of our traditions against fire, the most destructive force in the world." By this time, the priests had lowered the chest and slid it into the heart of the fire, which was held up by the structure built earlier. "The chest used to hold all of our most sacred relics from the time when we were a mighty kingdom, before we lost it all. Now there is only one relic left, a copy of an Endless Legend."

"Endless Legend?" Alexander rubbed his chin as if the term was familiar but could not remember it completely.

"It's a long story, but it's essentially an ancient scripture," Mira explained.

"Have you ever seen it?" Alexander asked.

"Certainly no! Only the Keeper can see it." Mira pointed to Gannon, who was overseeing the ceremony. "If anyone was to touch it who wasn't blessed as the sacred, why, their hands would be burned off by the divine."

Alexander pondered such power while Dresden scrunched his face at the perceived absurdity, but not without taking a quick glance at his hands. Dresden stopped himself from making a comment and went back to listening.

"Now The Keeper will say the blessing and the fire will consume the chest. Of course, the chest can withstand fire and protect everything inside."

"What's the point of all of this?" Alexander asked.

"Well, it's mostly symbolic, really. The elaborate structure of firewood represents the grandeur and complexity that our society had in the past. The fire, as you can really feel from being this close, represents the destruction that our people went through. Soon, this pyre will fall and turn into nothing but ash. The only thing that will remain will be the chest that holds the relics, which represents our fundamental values that we base our identity on. Without it, we don't have anything left that binds us to our ancestors."

"Tragic," Alexander commented.

"Actually, quite the opposite," Mira countered. "I look at it as encouraging. There really isn't much tradition left in this world that carries on through such hardship. The fact that we are still going on, despite everything, gives me hope."

"Hope for what?" Alexander asked.

"Hope that life will go on and find some way."

The ceremony continued, with the priests giving their sermons in their ancestral tongue while the fire consumed the pyre and the chest remained uncompromised. Mira continued telling different stories about where and how her people traveled throughout the world. Her society was one that did not have a goal or destination to reach; instead, they were people who believed they were destined to keep the light of civilization from burning out.

Alexander tried to understand more about the world. He wanted to know about these places, Oren and Acropoli. Dresden and Mira took turns to explain what they knew about them. Mira was not as knowledgeable about the conflict as Dresden due to his personal experience with seeing and meeting refugees along the road. Mira, however, had the unique experience of traveling across abandoned battlefields as her people searched for new places to call home, temporarily. The measure of destruction was unimaginable by Alexander's standard. Mountains and hills were made into barren plains, rivers and streams diverted, lakes drained, craters where whole towns once existed, and so much more.

Alexander wondered how such things could be happening without any possibility of coming to an end. The cruelty that he witnessed in the previous settlement made him believe that whatever war was being fought was far from over.

When the priests finished their part in the act, the ceremony transitioned into a more joyful event with music and dancing. Alexander took part in the celebrations with Mira at his side, giving him direction about the customs. The people, once distant, fell over each other in an attempt to introduce themselves to the proclaimed Holy Warden.

Alexander tried his luck at the traditional dances with varied success. These people were the first to show some measure of happiness in this world.

In another part of the festival, Dresden found himself at a tent serving alcohol and took part in sampling the more exotic of the concoctions.

Alexander eventually wandered back to the fire to observe the chest as it survived the intense flames. The heat made him sweat through every pore of his body, but even with the heat and the windless weather, a cold chill crawled up Alexander's, body making the hairs stand on end. Then, in the distance, a faint cry could be heard at the edge of town. That cry grew louder as it approached…

CHAPTER 13
A WARDEN'S WRATH

The crowd rushed to the commotion. Alexander pushed through the crowd to see what was going on. At the center of the crowd lay a wounded soldier, one of the town's guards. The man's body was ripped and bloodied from some kind of vicious ordeal. Around him, soldiers dressed in dark gray armor showed signs of wear from potentially the same ordeal.

Mira was on the ground, holding the wounded man in her arms as he forced what few whispered words he could get out. By this time, Dresden and Gannon had made their way to the center of the crowd. The wounded man finished his words to Mira before his body relaxed into a lifeless limp. Mira lowered her head and gently closed his eyes while she rested his head on the ground.

"Roamers?" Gannon asked Mira.

She shook her head. "Jackals."

The crowd grew restless with cries and yells of vengeance. Alexander noticed that Dresden stood silently off to the side with his hands on his hips. Gannon gestured to the crowd for calm as he called the rest of the guards forward.

A towering individual dressed in armor similar to Mira's stopped in front of Gannon, who acknowledged him as the leader of the guard and directed his attention to him.

"Drakus. How bad is it?" Gannon asked.

"Your eminence," Drakus replied. "We have reports that several patrols spotted a horde of these bastards heading this way. They appear to be organized in their movements, and well-armed."

"Organization?" Mira pondered. "That isn't natural."

"I sensed that something unnatural was afoot. Whatever is organizing them is after something," Gannon said.

"Or someone," Drakus suggested as he turned his gaze toward the Warden.

"We knew the risks when we took him in," Gannon responded.

"You should have just let them go!" Drakus argued. "We said that he would attract attention."

"It was a chance we had to take; I told you what the stakes were in my sermons."

"Bah, those damn visions of yours! I knew they would eventually drive us to ruin. Not on my watch. We're locking this place down," Drakus asserted.

"Drakus!" Mira yelled. "His eminence is the leader of our people. He will make the call as to what is best for our people."

"He is in charge of our souls, Mira. I am in charge of keeping us alive. I thought I made this clear. Until he and the priests take up arms in our defense, then we warriors are the ones who will call the shots in this situation. Now you can either fall in line or be a volunteer for a one-man recon!"

Mira stood down from Drakus and he took control of the situation. The crowd was ordered back to their homes and all soldiers were to prepare defenses around the town's entrance and other key points.

"The only way in is through the main entrance. The rest of this place is surrounded by mountains so treacherous not even Jackals can get through them. Call back all the patrols and call up any able-bodied male who can hold a sword or firearm." Then Drakus dismissed the soldiers to spread the word and prepare the defenses.

"What about me?" Mira asked.

"You? You can defend his holiness over there and his friends," Drakus remarked in annoyance as he pointed to Alexander and Dresden.

Mira sighed at her assignment but took it in stride as best she could. As the crowd dispersed, Drakus left to go oversee the preparations, issuing more orders over a device connected to larger piece of equipment on another soldier's back. Alexander inquired about the device to which Dresden explained it was a radio, like the one they saw from that first patrol. It had the capability to send voice messages over large distances, a fact that Alexander briefly marveled at. The town frantically prepared for the coming danger. Dresden stood by and watched the events unfold as Mira tried to direct Alexander to a safe place.

"Pointless to hide," Dresden said. "We have to fight; we'll die, but better than dying like a coward."

"I don't know if you have heard of these things, but—" Mira started.

"I have encountered these *people* before. Dangerous and wild with no fear of death. Unorganized they are deadly. Organized? I can only imagine that they are downright unstoppable," Dresden said.

"Then might as well fight," Gannon interjected with a focus placed on Alexander. "Wardens are the protectors, they do not need protecting."

"No pressure then," Dresden said sarcastically to a wide-eyed Alexander.

Alexander's body shook from the pressure placed on him. He regained himself and let out a deep breath. "Better go fetch my gear then."

As he reached the tent a soft whisper echoed in his ear, carried by the same chill he felt before. "*Warden.*"

Alexander shivered as he looked over his shoulder to find that no one was there. He grabbed his gear and rushed back to the center of town where Dresden and Mira were waiting. They all decided to join the rest of the defenders at the front line. Mira, armed with her sword, grabbed a rifle from one of the nearby armories on the way.

At the gate, the defenders set up several rudimentary barricades and positioned themselves so they had cover. The soldiers focused their attention on the tree line ahead, and used the surrounding buildings as a way of covering their flanks. Dresden looked around and scoffed at some of the positions the soldiers were taking. Vantage points were overlooked, men were spread out, alleyways were lightly covered, and everyone was on the ground rather than elevated positions.

"They think they are fighting a stand-up fight. This will be a massacre," Dresden remarked as he turned to Mira. "Your commander is going to get us all killed."

Mira listened to what Dresden had to say about the deficiencies and then searched for Drakus to have him change his strategy. Drakus stormed over in a fury.

"What are you doing up here? I told you to protect these two! That doesn't mean bring them up to the meat grinder!" Drakus raged.

"I'm afraid this is going to be a meat grinder, all right, just not in the way you might hope," Dresden countered.

"What are you talking about?" Drakus demanded.

"He means to say that the strategy here is ill equipped to take on a horde of Jackals, sir," Mira explained.

Dresden cleared his throat. "You see, the men need to be more closely bunched in order to create a line of fire that—"

"I don't need advice from some outsider who hides behind a mask," Drakus scoffed as he turned to Mira. "Or a woman, for that matter. If you all want to help, then take up a position and try your best to stay out of the way."

"Listen to me, you idiot, these men are going to die because of your stupidity unless you take advice from those who actually have seen whole units destroyed by these things!" Dresden yelled.

"I'll have you shot for such insolen—"

Drakus' rant was interrupted by a distress call over the radio from a nearby patrol. The voices screamed in terror as the sounds of static and howling took over until the signal went dead. Just then, the sound of something fast approaching came from the forest.

Everyone's attention was turned to the source of the noise. Dresden, Mira, and Alexander took positions as Drakus slowly moved to a barricade. He attempted to try to reach the other patrols on the radio, but to no avail.

The bushes and branches snapped and shook so much that they became the loudest sound in the entire area. A soldier next to Alexander violently flinched in a way that caused everyone around him to react as if something had snuck up on them. However, the cause of the frightened twitch was only a raindrop.

One drop turned into many and soon became a downpour. The view of the tree line began to slip behind the rain with only the occasional lightning flash to show what lay beyond. The situation was not ideal. All around them, the men wore a look of panic on their faces. The buildings beside them felt more like menacing walls preventing escape rather than offering protection. The alleyways that separated the buildings were dark and covered only by a handful of troops. Rifles, swords, axes, and other types of weapons were peppered throughout the ranks as they sat in wait. Those with rifles actively shared ammo with one another to balance out the strength of the lines.

Alexander moved to one of the alleys that appeared to be undermanned. Placing himself behind the makeshift barricade with two other soldiers, he observed that the alley was still lit by a lone torch in the distance. The rain had reduced the flame to a flicker, but it still went on. That same cold breeze once again crawled over Alexander's skin.

A crash came from behind the lines as a wooden cart collapsed; the noise caused nearly everyone to turn around to see what it was. In another instant, the sound of movement intensified from the tree line, which caused another shift in attention. In rapid succession, loud thuds, muffled by the rain and thunder, were heard on the surrounding rooftops. Footsteps, growls, hisses, and other noises echoed all around them.

Alexander looked all around for the noises, but when he looked back down his alley, he saw a lone dark silhouette in the distance. In the blink of an eye, the torch was extinguished. Shocked, Alexander moved back to where Dresden and Mira were. He drew his weapons and sat in anticipation for what was about to come.

"You look like you saw a ghost," Dresden commented.

"I wish I had," Alexander muttered.

A scream from the town behind them pierced through the air and made everyone's hair stand on end. Drakus moved around in confusion as the sounds of other sentries began to light up the radio with shooting and frantic calls. He tried to get through the noise to issue orders, but a lone voice took over the radio.

The sound started as static, but intensified to the menacing groan of a person who was more like a wild animal. The groan grew in volume to the point where everyone could hear it despite Drakus' attempts to lower the volume. The moan suddenly stopped and there was an eerie silence that was ended by a response that haunted every soul that heard it.

"You… should… have… stayed."

Alexander's eyes widened. A soldier was jerked instantly into a dark alley, another followed, and calls came out that men were missing.

Then they came. Out of all corners and directions, they came. Wild, mangled, and rabid men and women rushed out and attacked everyone they saw. Hunched in their stance, the Jackals were like animals in their speed and vicious nature. Barely clothed, these things attacked with their hands, teeth, and whatever weapons they held.

"There they go over there, get them, GET THEM!" one solider yelled as he engaged his targets with his rifle.

"They're all over the place!" another yelled.

A hail of gunfire went in every direction. Ranged combat was quickly reduced to hand-to-hand combat as the Jackals closed the distance. Order in the lines gave to disorder as men shouted orders to fall back while some lost their nerve and went on ill-advised rampages that left them alone and surrounded.

Mira lunged at the first Jackal who came near Alexander as Dresden used his blade to cut down one that came from the rooftop. The perimeter was barely reordered as the men became frantic in their fight to beat back the enemy. In the swarm, Alexander found himself face to face with a Jackal who had finished off another soldier. Covered in blood and foaming at the mouth, it lunged at him, only to be stopped by his shield. The force briefly disoriented the Jackal, but it made another lunge at Alexander, knocking him to the ground. The broad side of his blade held up the Jackal as it tried to bite and scratch the air between them.

Unsure of what to do, Alexander was saved by Dresden's blade, which pierced through the face of the Jackal from behind. He discarded the body as Dresden stood above him.

"Butter knives…" Dresden remarked before helping him up. "There's too many of them, we got to—"

A Jackal tackled Dresden before he could react. Alexander took his blade and instinctively thrust it into the back of the Jackal, which caused it to howl and convulse. Another blow by Alexander finished it off, to Dresden's surprise.

However, what happened next shocked Alexander even more. His sword-bearing hand began to writhe in seething pain. Dropping his weapon, he saw a faint outline of a marking appear on his palm until it disappeared along with the pain.

Dresden noticed there was something wrong with Alexander, but did not say anything as he handed him his weapon.

"Never hesitate," Dresden advised as he turned to the center of town where there was some activity near the bonfire. "There's trouble in town."

"The temple!" Mira shouted.

Alexander and Dresden followed her closely as the Jackals continued their assault. The flow of enemies from the alleyways was stopped by some soldiers who lit them on fire with incendiaries. The act allowed the rest of soldiers to fall back without the worry of being surrounded.

Smoke filled the air, causing the rest of the soldiers to slowly fall back to let the Jackals be the only ones to suffocate. The three had to fight their way through several Jackals to get to the temple. Alexander was mindful about what happened when he killed before, so he was using his shield as a means of knocking away enemies rather than killing them.

Meanwhile, inside the temple, Gannon knelt at the altar in silent prayer. The room was alight by numerous candles in front and decorated with colorful parchments that pictured various myths from the past.

The sound of the distant battle was faint compared to the roar the bonfire still projected. Gannon's simple white robe was stained with sweat as the heat sweltered in the room. His hands crossed and head bowed, Gannon silently lipped the prayers of his ancestors in dialects both known and unknown.

Amidst the heat and sounds of war and rain, the air turned stale and quiet. Gannon opened his eyes and raised his head when he felt the change. His skin grew tight and his breath visible; the air was frigid. With a sense of calm, Gannon stood up and turned around to see a figure before him. The figure stood silent as its face was hidden behind the shadow of its dark attire. Its hands were crossed in front, one over one the other under the long sleeves.

"I'm quite surprised really," Gannon spoke. "That you would give a pawn like me the personal attention of the man behind the strings."

"No man." The figure spoke in a deep raspy voice.

"Of course, an insult I'm sure. I have seen you before, a shadow that lurks in my dreams, symbolizing the nightmare that we all live in and even the fears of something far worse. Might think of yourself as a mystery, but I know who you are," Gannon said to the figure, which prompted its head to tilt in curiosity. "And what you plan to do."

Alexander and the others reached the outside of the temple and turned to engage the Jackals who pursued them. Dresden and Mira cut down their few as Alexander punched and kicked a Jackal. Unable to knock the Jackal out, Alexander pushed it into the bonfire with his shield. To his displeasure, the fiery death brought another sharp pain to his hand that brought the symbol back briefly.

"Warden, go to the temple, we'll take care of them here," Mira instructed.

Dresden and Mira continued their fight as Alexander rushed inside. He felt the temperature change as he entered the main chamber of the building. There he witnessed the familiar dark figure snap Gannon's neck.

"No!" Alexander screamed. His grip tightened on his weapons when he charged the figure, only to be knocked away by a hidden Jackal. The force knocked Alexander down, but he regained himself fast enough to kill the Jackal, which brought back the brief, but seething pain. At that moment he noticed that the attack had knocked the compass out of his control. The figure picked up the compass and examined it before turning to Alexander.

"Foolish child," the figure said in a voice that sent a chill up Alexander's spine. It floated above the ground menacingly, projecting an almost alien aura that felt unnatural to this world, but there was something that made Alexander feel as though it was something or someone that still belongs to the realm of the living.

Alexander carefully moved around to find the perfect moment to strike. The figure paid no attention to Alexander, simply repositioned himself and continued to examine the compass.

"You aren't leaving here with that," Alexander said. "I won't let you."

The figure put the compass away in his cloak and then turned to Alexander. It crossed its hands again as its body continued its ghostly stance. "Then you will die."

Alexander readied his stance in anticipation. Dresden ran in behind him.

"What the hell is that?" Dresden asked, drawing his bloodied weapons.

Mira entered the room from the opposite side to see the figure, but the sight of Gannon's corpse brought tears to her eyes.

"Father!" Her cries attracted the attention of the figure.

Alexander charged at the distracted figure. The figure snapped its head back to Alexander, raised its hand, and projected a force that shot Alexander back like a bullet out of the temple, through the bonfire and into the wall of a nearby building.

It then countered Mira's blade with its own that came into existence the moment before Mira could strike. She was forced back across the room by a single strike. Dresden fired his pistol at the figure and struck it in the shoulder. The figure reacted slightly to the hit. In an instant, it disappeared in a puff of dark smoke. The cold subsided and the sounds of the outside world returned. Before rushing outside to find Alexander, Dresden helped up Mira, who pushed him aside to run to Gannon's body.

The bonfire had exploded from the impact of Alexander flying through it, littering flaming debris for a dozen feet in each direction.

By this time the rain had stopped, but the fighting continued around the town. Dresden noticed a large impact hole in one of the buildings and rushed to examine it. Alexander was on his knees with his head down. His chest puffed in and out with his heavy breathing.

"Alex?"

Alexander raised his head. His jaw was locked, his face etched with a look of intense hatred. Dresden, however, noticed something else; his eyes were changing. With every heavy breath, his eyes changed from blue to red. A boiling heat flowed through Alexander's veins as his vision fogged with a red haze. His hands clenched and muscles tightened in reaction to a numbness that made his skin crawl as if he was covered in daggers. All sorts of thoughts and voices echoed in his head, both familiar and unfamiliar. The voices echoed that he had been chosen, and he had been marked. Alexander examined his hand, which was the source of the mysterious symbol and noticed that it had returned, along with the burning sensation.

Distracted by the change Alexander was undergoing, Dresden was tackled by a Jackal. He found himself surrounded by three Jackals who had snuck up on him. His blades jammed and would not open properly, which forced him to use his fists. Dresden's efforts were not enough and he was soon overpowered and knocked to the ground.

A Jackal wielding an axe approached him and raised his weapon to strike. But before the Jackal could swing, its head was separated from its neck by the sword of the red-eyed Alexander. The remaining Jackals tried to rush him, but one was sliced in half and the other knocked through a wall from a shield hit. Dresden was shocked to see Alexander act in such a way; he would have been impressed if it was not so threatening.

Growls and howls came from behind them as several Jackals moved in, waiting to strike. In the blink of an eye, Alexander rushed them all and killed them in a fury of speed and brutality. Jackals were sliced, punched, and thrown around like rag dolls through buildings with the same force as if they had been fired from cannons.

One of them landed a blow to Alexander's back with an axe. Unfortunately for the Jackal, the axe's blade shattered when it struck the armor that now emanated a glow from beneath the torn cloak.

After striking down the Jackal, Alexander threw off his cloak to reveal elaborate armor that glowed in the chaos of battle. Scores of Jackals were obliterated in the onslaught, and Alexander started to feel a boost in his energy with every enemy he cut down. This high he felt appeared to be almost endless until he found the discipline to stop his assault.

During the rampage, Drakus came to help Dresden with a few soldiers and was shocked to see what Alexander had done. The remaining Jackals swarmed out of town at the sight of what had happened to the Jackals Alexander took on. With no more enemies left to fight, Alexander stood where he was with his victims lying all around. He pulled up his sleeve to look at the marking on his hand along with several expansions that spread up his arm like an elaborate tattoo. His eyes faded back to blue and the markings disappeared as the pain began to set in. The glow from his armor faded back to normal as he moved to recover his cloak.

The people began to come out of hiding. They did not seem happy or grateful for the victory; instead, they were hesitant and frightened by his fast, brutal and inhuman actions which were every bit as terrifying as what the jackals had done.

Alexander looked around at the people and saw the fear in their eyes as they stood by what remained of the homes destroyed in his rampage. The people had long-held beliefs about the Wardens and none of them seemed to expect what had happened. A quiet and reserved individual had switched to a cold-blooded killer who killed in a way never seen before. It was one thing to believe that someone like a Warden had incredible power, but it was another thing to see it. This was their Warden... quiet, unsure, and unpredictable.

CHAPTER 14
DEMON

The fires were extinguished, the rain had stopped, but the destruction remained. Citizens emerged from their shelters to find their streets covered in the rubble of various buildings. These people had witnessed the disasters and horrors of war, but this was different. As they cleaned up their settlement, serviced the dead, and comforted the wounded, a new reality unsettled their nerves.

The remains of the bonfire in front of the temple was cleared away to make room for the people to lay their dead in rows. Wrapped in plain white sheets, the dead consisted of both their people and the Jackals.

Dresden observed that the enemy corpses were treated kindly even though they had so recently been a murderous terror. Thunder continued to echo in the distance to the displeasure of the alert populace. Families grieved over their lost loved ones in different ways. Some cried, others stood silent, while a few lost their senses in their grief. Dresden went back into the temple to find several priests and Mira huddled around the altar that bore Gannon's body. Mira stood silently over the body, her glazed eyes staring fixedly into the face of her slain father. Upon seeing Dresden, the priests moved away to talk amongst themselves.

"What are they so secretive about?" Dresden asked.

"Probably just debating on who will succeed my father. Grief is a short process for the ambitious," Mira said.

"Hm, people seem to be a little on edge out there. You think they'd be a little more comforted since the remaining patrols came back to reinforce the place."

"They have had their hearts ripped out. First their leader was taken." Mira turned to the sight of the chest that was broken open by Alexander's impact. "Then, their history was shown to be a lie."

Dresden paused to choose his words carefully. "What do you mean, a lie?"

"There was nothing in that chest."

"Oh, yeah there was, I saw what was in it, the Endless Legend inscription," Dresden said to an unconvinced Mira. "It's true! Your father showed it to me before the ceremony."

"Even if that is true, why would he show someone like you and how come you still have your hands?"

"Well, about that whole hands would burn off part, like you said before, perhaps some stories become diluted. In any case, he showed it to me to try and keep me from leaving after I found out what Alex's real mission was."

"What almost made you leave?"

"The guy wants to resurrect his girlfriend's soul from The Abyss."

"So, the Legend is true, just like father said."

"I remember it being a little more ambiguous than the certainty you're throwing around."

"Without the Warden it would be hard to understand, but his presence and true purpose here are too much to be a mere coincidence," Mira argued.

"In any event, Alex's journey has brought us up against something that is part of a force that can't be trifled with. His *performance* during the battle adds a little more complexity to it; I think he might be getting in over his head."

"How do you mean?"

"Something about when he killed that one Jackal; there was something off about it. Moreover, his little rampage… he fought like a man possessed."

"You think he will be all right?"

"I'll let you know as soon as he turns up."

A group of soldiers marched into the temple with Drakus close behind, with orders being shouted to secure the building. The priests expressed their dissatisfaction with the presence of armed men inside the sacred place, but they were silenced as Drakus explained the situation to them before he turned to the others at the altar.

"Not one Jackal remains in the area," Drakus stated.

"Since when do Jackals retreat?" Mira asked.

"They don't, that's the thing," Dresden said.

"Where is the Warden?" Drakus asked quickly.

"We're not sure. He disappeared after the battle, didn't say anything to us," Mira said.

"Well, that being the case, the Warden presents a significant security risk at the moment," Drakus explained.

"A risk? The Warden just saved us from the jackals, surely you're overreacting," Mira said.

Drakus scratched the back of his head and paced around the altar. He glanced at the body of Gannon and the overturned chest that used to hold their most sacred relic. A loud sigh came from Drakus when he turned back to them.

"We've been devastated, that we cannot overlook. Our leader is dead and our relics are gone. The community is more vulnerable to destruction than it has ever been in my lifetime," Drakus said.

"We are vulnerable, but the Warden protected us," Mira said.

"The scriptures never told us that a Warden can wield such power!" one of the priests yelled. "There was never an indication that becoming a red-eyed demon was part of being a Warden!"

"Maybe your scriptures are wrong," Dresden suggested with a sense of annoyance at the sound of a religious argument.

"Bah!" the priest balked.

"What are you suggesting?" Mira asked.

"He is no Warden! He is a demon!" another priest yelled to the agreement of the others.

Drakus turned to gesture silence to the group of priests, but he was not able to silence their shouts. The guards were on edge as the priests continued to shout in their religious language at the group.

"You can't possibly be in the same camp as these fanatics?" Dresden suggested to Drakus.

"I'm not troubling myself with the dogmatic concerns surrounding the Warden. Demon or no, you can't deny that his display of power was something that cannot be controlled," Drakus said.

"By you," Dresden said.

"By anyone, himself perhaps," Drakus countered.

"He seemed in control enough to only kill Jackals," Dresden argued.

"You saw outside?" Drakus pointed out the door to the display of bodies. "A handful were killed by Jackals. The rest were found under the rubble of buildings damaged by the actions of the Warden. He didn't think that throwing bodies like a cannon into buildings full of people would be a problem. Either he did know, or he didn't care."

"Or didn't know his own power?" Mira said.

"Just as bad a case, if not worse. If he didn't know about his power, then how can we say he can control it?" Drakus suggested.

"A difficult situation," Dresden added.

"Indeed, it is. I ordered the guard to search the entire area for the Warden," Drakus said.

"For what possible purpose?" Mira asked.

Drakus sighed. "We must make sure he doesn't cause anymore inadvertent harm."

"He could easily be spoken to without the use of guns and soldiers," Dresden said. "Unless you don't plan to have a long conversation?"

"I have to do what I must to protect our people. If we find the Warden and he doesn't leave, then we have no choice but to—"

"I'll save you the trouble. I'll find him and get him out of here," Dresden interrupted.

"*We* will," Mira added to the surprised men. "Sir, my purpose is with the lasting wish of my father. With his vision for the Warden, the Legend, and—"

"You seek vengeance, Mira," Drakus interrupted. "Against the shadow that took your father."

"It murdered him, Drakus," she said. "Whether you believe it or not."

"After the events of the last day, I'll have to take your word about the shadow demon. I don't believe the Warden did this to him, but he is operating on a level that is beyond us. And on that level, he will bring things that we cannot imagine, and thought were long dead. I only hope that you can keep him from bringing the collateral damage of his journey to us normal folk around the world."

"That I promise, sir," Mira swore.

"Sir!" a scout yelled as he ran into the temple. "There's something approaching the town!

CHAPTER 15
HAVEN

Alexander darted down an alleyway as the sound of marching footsteps approached from the main street. He entered through a conveniently ajar door and locked it behind him. The room was dark, but he furiously moved to block the door with whatever he could find. When the room was finally secured, someone lit a candle across the room, startling him. There, a middle-aged woman sat with her young son. As the boy crouched in terror at the sight of the intruder, the woman seemed unnerved by his presence. He held up his hands to gesture that he did not mean them harm.

"What do you want, Warden?" the woman questioned.

"I just need to lay low for right now."

"Why? Is someone looking for you?"

Alexander scratched the back of his head. "I'm not sure."

"Then why are you hiding?"

"Appears as though I might have unnerved you all from my actions. But, you seem to be rather calm."

"Well, that's probably because I just don't frankly care for your presence," the woman bluntly said.

"I apologize for my intrusion."

"Think you can just waltz into any place you want because you're some divine figure?"

"No! I don't agree with the assertion that—wait, you don't think of me as some holy piece of the divine like everyone else?"

"Bah!" the woman scoffed as she tapped her child to go into the other room, "That whole hocus pocus stuff might be for them, but none of that nonsense for me."

"So, you don't think I'm a Warden?"

"Oh, you could be someone from that cockamamie place in the sky, but that doesn't make you holy."

"Oh, that's actually a tad refreshing." Alexander grabbed his arm, which was sore from the burning sensation that flared up during battle. The woman thought he was injured, so she sat him down to treat him. "It's nothing, really."

"Oh, that's what they all say," she mocked as she found nothing wrong with him. "Ah, there really is nothing. Then what's wrong with you? Don't be carrying on like you haven't got a set, son."

"Not sure how to answer any of that."

"They never do."

An examination of the room by Alexander had him scratching his head. The only decoration was several crude drawings of trees. The whole room was covered in these dark colored pictures.

"All these pictures," he said as the woman glared, "They're nice."

She huffed. "My kid drew them."

"Ah, well, yeah, they're nice. Really nice."

"Oh, stop with the hollow compliments."

"Must admit, not really as welcoming as the others I've met here."

"Helps when you're not from here."

"Where are you from?" Alexander asked, but the conversation was cut short by a knock at the door and the sound of men.

The woman approached the door and answered them through the door rather than opening it. The town guard asked if everything was all right. The woman answered in the affirmative and asked that they go away. Before leaving, the men asked if she had seen the Warden around the town. Despite her inquires, they would not give a reason as to why they were searching for him. Alexander looked at her with a look of desperation and after a moment of thought, she said that she had not seen the Warden. He was relieved to hear the guards leave. The woman sighed and brought him some water as he sat with his head in his hands.

"They must be desperate for some kind of blessing from you or something," the woman suggested.

"Not exactly, I think I showed them something they didn't expect from me."

"Well, you appear harmless enough. Originally, I'm from a small town called Ollen a bit out of the way from here. Decided that it was best to get my children out of town before the war eventually made its way to us."

"Did it?"

"From what I heard, yes. We roamed around the wilderness for a while until I shacked up with some fellow refugees. They ended up taking us to some city, Haven. From there, we ended up here once we realized it wasn't safe. We were lucky to get out the way we did."

"Seems like you made it fine, since you're here in this relatively *safe* place," Alexander commented as he continued looking around the room. "Your son is a vivid artist."

"Those were all actually my daughter's doing. She was the artist of the family. Drew everything she saw."

All the pictures were the same, each a dark forest of some kind. However, Alexander stopped when he stumbled across one picture that stuck out from the rest. Instead of a collection of lines that resembled trees, this one was structures that gave the impression of a city. Alexander looked around at the furnishings in the room and noticed a faceless doll with long blond hair and a dirty white dress sitting on the couch. He picked up the doll, then noticed something on the dress that caused him to put the doll down and turn to the woman.

"What happened to your daughter?"

"It was stupid of me to think that place was safe. When we realized the city was essentially a shooting gallery, we grouped up with some others who had the same idea. We had to use the alleyways and avoid the streets since the place was crawling with snipers. Did pretty well up until we reached a main road we had to cross. It made sense to wait for dark, but the place was getting so bad that our group leader couldn't wait anymore. I took my son, while another adult took my daughter since they thought I would be too slow if I ran with both of them. I went first, made it across, no problem. My daughter went after me with a man who carried her." She paused. "I didn't see the shot, but I'll never forget the sound that took them both down. The man died instantly, but my little girl was still alive with a bullet wound in her stomach."

"Wh—"

"Couldn't do anything," she continued before he could ask. "If I had gone out there, I would have died and my boy would have lost his mother. The group would have surely left him if I were dead. Instead, I just had to sit there. They decided to wait for nightfall since they thought going forward was too dangerous. Too dangerous… ironic." The woman closed her eyes. "She wailed as the street filled with her blood. 'Mommy, mommy,' that's all she said. Didn't have any other thought in the world than to just see me. Went on for what felt like hours until she finally had no more left in her... no more blood, no more cries, no more. I never cried after that. Nothing I'll ever witness could hurt that much."

Alexander tried to utter words, but was not able to muster enough of a breath to say anything.

"So why did you end up visiting our wonderful little Hell down here, Warden?"

Before Alexander could speak, they were interrupted by the raucous soldiers running outside towards an ever-growing roar of grinding metal.

CHAPTER 16
THE HARVEST DAWN

A tense standoff is the best way to describe the situation. Soldiers of the town stood at attention with their weapons at the low ready. In front of them was a contingent of foreign soldiers accompanied by two tanks that had their turrets aimed at the town. Drakus hurried to the front with Dresden and Mira in tow. Dressed in gray uniforms, the visitors were more relaxed in their stance compared to the local forces. In an effort to keep the situation from escalating, Drakus signaled his men to stand down.

"What's going on here?" Drakus turned to one of his lieutenants. "How did they get this close without us knowing?"

"You ordered back all the patrols to reinforce the town, sir," the officer whispered.

"Shit, that's right." Drakus turned to the visitors. "What's your business? Come for a fight?"

A man urged his horse forward and stopped in front of Drakus. "If we wanted a fight, I assure you we wouldn't be this close. Makes a mess of things."

"You in charge?" Drakus asked.

"Aye, Captain Ostro of Acropoli. These are my scouts; we monitor this sector after wresting it from Termina and those chaotic

Municipalities." Ostro's gaze swept over the settlement, "I wasn't aware there was a settlement here. Maps don't show anything."

"We're a people on the move," Drakus told him.

"Ah, nomads," Ostro commented.

"We are not nomads, sir."

The two went back and forth over the word that caused offense for an inordinate amount of time. Dresden took a hard look around at the men they faced down and then turned his attention to the buildings. Upon one of the rooftops, he noticed Alexander peeking over a wall. There was something off about his gaze. Alexander glared menacingly at Ostro. Dresden looked back at Ostro, who had a white beard and wore a helmet that covered the rest of his features.

I know this man…

"Nomads or not, whichever," Ostro declared. "You all are welcome to stay within the boundaries of the Acropoli Kingdom."

"Oh, we appreciate the honor, for sure. What brought you out here? A little heavy for a scouting unit."

"We heard what sounded like a battle from our encampment. Thought we'd investigate, since a fight on our lands is of interest to us."

"Sorry to say, you missed the battle. Would have been nice to have those tanks of yours with us, but doubt they would have helped against a horde of Jackals."

"Jackals did this?" Ostro asked with astonishment.

"They were organized, came on us under the cover of a storm. Got dicey, but they were repelled."

"Organized Jackals? Never thought I'd hear that. Well then, you all should be commended. Surely, your defense kept those things from attacking an innocent settlement."

"We appreciate the commendation."

"However, the news of organized Jackals running around in the area is something I can't ignore. I'll be sending help to reinforce this area."

"Oh, no that isn't necessary, sir—"

"I insist, good sir," Ostro interrupted. "In the next week, I'll have a company up here to establish a base and operation center in your settlement. We can never be too careful."

"What if we don't need your help?"

"Then I'm sure you can find more land to squat on elsewhere." Ostro signaled to the group and the tanks roared to life. "In any event, we'll go see if we can't mop up any more of these Jackals. See you all soon, good day to you."

Drakus could not get a word in before the group started to march off. All he could do was watch as Ostro turned back, removed his helmet, and gave a salutation to Drakus.

From Dresden's vantage point he was surprised to see Ostro's features. Something about his bald head and the scar on his face seemed familiar. He turned to look for Alexander and found him missing from his spot on the roof. *Oh shit. What's he up to now?*

The exit of the Acropoli soldiers went without incident as Drakus dispersed his men to various positions to watch out for any more visitors. Once the area was deemed secure from any further intrusions, Drakus and the others went back to the temple in the center of town where the atmosphere became even more tense than before. Dresden struggled to find the right moment to announce his realization that Alexander might be out for revenge against the Acropoli captain. The priests voiced their dismay at the news that foreign soldiers were going to occupy their settlement.

"It's an annexation!" one priest shouted.

"Aye, it will mark the beginning of the end for our culture," another announced.

Drakus could do little to calm their fears. No doubt his mannerisms and frustration gave away the impression that he, himself, was left without answers.

Mira sensed something was wrong with Dresden and finally got him to speak after enough prodding. The room's attention turned to him when Mira announced he had something important to say.

"We might have a bigger issue on our hands," Dresden stated.

"What issue might that be?" Drakus asked.

"The man, Ostro, was it? I recognize him." Dresden struggled to piece together his story. "When Alex first arrived, we found ourselves at a town some ways from here. The town was attacked by Acropoli and they destroyed it. No survivors. Ostro led the massacre."

The revelation caused the room to erupt in frantic bits of conversation laced with fear and paranoia. Drakus put a hand up, asking for silence.

"I have no doubt that Alex remembers the man. I saw him glaring at him from the rooftops, and then he disappeared. That massacre shook him up pretty bad, not something I think he would forget." Dresden explained.

"Are you suggesting—"

"He's going to try and kill him. Possibly his soldiers as well," Dresden interrupted Drakus. "After everything he's seen, I have no doubt that the world might be getting to him. With his newfound *abilities*, it's easy to think that he might try and use them to get some kind of revenge."

"Why are you sure he will lash out?" Mira asked.

"What we witnessed was not easy to see. For me, it wasn't anything new, but that was the first time he ever witnessed such violence. When someone watches a child get executed for no reason, there is a good chance that person won't flinch at the opportunity for revenge," Dresden explained.

"For the love of the Gods, he'll kill us all!" a priest yelled to Drakus.

"He's right," Drakus agreed. "Destruction of that unit will only invite retribution. And since they might not be keen on accepting that a Warden did it, they will probably blame us."

"I'm going after him," Dresden said. "I can try and stop him."

"Even if you do succeed, I can't allow our people to become subjects to Acropoli." Drakus turned to his senior officers. "We're leaving, now."

"Leaving?" Mira questioned. "We can't leave yet; our scouts haven't found a new site yet!"

"We'll backtrack to our former settlement; it's dangerous, but no more than being here to suffer subjection or death. Leave the buildings. Don't break them down. We'll build new ones. We leave at dawn."

Priests, soldiers, and anyone else in the room moved immediately to their tasks. The priests began collecting valuables as the soldiers spread the word and began to help break down the settlement. The series of movements appeared to have been executed many times before to become a seamless art. Within a few minutes, the seemingly settled town was ready to migrate as tents were torn down and carts filled with belongings. No one griped or protested the move; it was a part of their lives and considering recent events, might be the desired choice.

Mira tried to negotiate a better place to move, but Drakus would not budge on his decision.

"None of this matters if that unit out there gets killed. We'll have an entire kingdom looking for us. We'd never be safe." Drakus walked to the map brought in by his officers.

"Not unless we stop him," Dresden suggested.

"It'll have to be you. Can't spare any of my men, and they'd probably get killed by the Warden before they could stop him. You, on the other hand, might be able to talk him down," Drakus conceded before he turned to Mira. "Go with him, Mira."

"Consider it done; we'll stop him. I'll try to find a new place for our people, a safe place, one we can call home," Mira promised.

"If you can do that, then I'd be grateful. Until then, good luck." Drakus saluted.

"Just a quick question before we go," Dresden said. "That map you've got there. Have any copies you'd be able to spare?"

"No, this is our only copy."

"Ah, damn, all right then," Dresden said before the two went off in search of Alexander.

The column of soldiers marched down the dirt road to the pace of the tanks that churned through the fresh mud. Hills surrounded the road and the endless sea of trees created a barrier of darkness that was difficult to see through.

In that darkness, Alexander hid, watched and waited. He moved from tree to tree, stone to stone, or whatever kept him concealed when the column stopped to patrol the surrounding area. Ostro went up and down the lines, conversing from time to time with his men, sharing an occasional joke. The cloak Alexander wore to conceal his foreign equipment became an impediment to his attempt at remaining hidden as it caught various branches and rock edges. He removed the cloak, tossed it aside, and continued to follow the soldiers. His armor had become dirty from the journey, and his sword still bore the dark brown stains of blood. The shield had suffered in the previous night's battle, but the blue and yellow eagle remained prominent and easily recognizable. Alexander's movements gave the impression of a predator stalking prey, but at each moment of opportunity, he hesitated and let the chance slip away.

Farther down the road, the group finally came to a halt as a downed tree blocked their path. As the soldiers prepared to move the tree, the moment to strike had finally arrived. But, as Alexander positioned himself behind a large boulder, his foot snapped a branch and caught the attention of a soldier. He cursed himself silently as the soldier came closer to investigate the noise. His sword and shield at the ready, Alexander gripped his weapons tight and shook with nerves. The sound of the soldier's footsteps got louder. Alexander took a deep breath and jumped up with his weapons ready to strike but stopped at the sight of the soldier.

"A kid," Alexander said in shock as the child soldier stood there with a look of confusion.

The moment of pause was broken by an arrow that pierced the eye of the child soldier, killing him. More arrows came out of the surrounding forest, harassing the rest of the soldiers on the road and throwing them into a state of frantic confusion. Many of them were unable to get a shot off before they were cut down by the silent death that came with a well-placed arrow to the head.

Ostro went into a craze, shouting for his men to open fire at the shadowy figures on the other side of the road Alexander saw as he took cover. Large boulders rolled out of the forest down the hill into the frenzied formation on the road. Men were crushed by the immense rocks as a few slammed into the sides of the tanks, exploding one of them. The explosion caused Ostro's horse to buck, throwing him to the ground. The crew from the remaining tank exited their vehicle in an attempt to flee, but were cut down by arrows.

A group of ironclad warriors streamed out of the wood line, bearing large shields and wielding strange-looking rifles that shot arrows instead of bullets. The warriors used their shield to deflect the desperate shots that came from the remaining soldiers. In an impressive display of synchronization, the warriors combined their shields to protect themselves from the volley of gunfire as they closed the distance. Once close enough, they broke ranks into a charge with swords and a thunderous roar that struck visible fear into the remaining soldiers. It was no contest as the warriors finished up whoever was left standing on the road. When the last one was cut down, the group celebrated their victory. With their armor and bearded faces, these mysterious warriors appeared gargantuan and vicious. Suddenly Alexander felt a cold, sharp sting on his neck.

"Drop your weapons!" a warrior ordered from behind with his sword to his neck.

After a moment of thought, Alexander dropped his weapons and followed the orders of the warrior. Another warrior grabbed his arms and tied his hands together. He was forced down the hill where the rest of the group rummaged through the equipment of their fallen foes. The sight of Alexander caught the attention of several the warriors, who paused what they were doing to analyze their new prisoner. He was brought in front of a warrior dressed in elaborate armor and an orange cape that symbolized authority.

"Sir, we captured this one on the outskirts, spying on us," the warrior explained. "He was armed with these."

The warrior dropped Alexander's sword and shield before the leader of the group. He examined the equipment for a brief moment before losing interest.

"Expected to do much with these?" the leader asked a silent Alexander. "Not much of a talker? Well, you're not one of these bastards from the look of your armor."

The leader's attention was drawn away by the arrival of another prisoner, Ostro. He struggled against the warriors before being thrown to his knees next to Alexander. They shared a glance before turning to face the leader.

"Take it this was your outfit of hardened warriors?" the leader asked Ostro.

"I'm sorry; I only talk to those who offer the courtesy of sharing their name," Ostro barked back.

"Temperamental, aren't we? From your position, I'd show a little more respect," the leader suggested. "But, if it pains you that much, my blessed name is Aeneas and these are my warriors of the Harvest Dawn."

"Oh, yeah, I've heard about you. Just my luck to be captured by a bunch of crazed cultists. You do realize you just attacked the Acropoli Kingdom and all her allies?"

"Yes, yes, yes, I've heard this song and dance before. The Princely Municipalities, Terrani, Orenians, all the different ones. We've been offending a lot of people these days," Aeneas quipped.

"Butchered my men, stripped them of their belongings, why don't you just kill me already?"

"Rather wasteful right now, could be of some use."

"I'll never talk!"

"Nor do you have to, just keep quiet for now and be a good boy," Aeneas said as he turned to Alexander. "You, on the other hand. What use are you to me?"

Alexander remained silent, and Aeneas' frustration grew. He began to fiddle with Alexander's shield. Out of curiosity, he flipped it over and saw the eagle symbol on the other side. The warriors who witnessed the reveal gasped at the sight of the symbol, some immediately dropping to their knees in submission. Aeneas took a step back after seeing the eagle, but regained his composure. The warriors' reaction confused both Alexander and Ostro.

"What? It's just a bird," Ostro said, bemused.

"So, the damned thing was right," Aeneas said. "Well, I guess you, sir, have just said everything you needed to without a word."

Aeneas instructed his guards to cut the restraints on Alexander and ordered that the group prepare to leave. Alexander's sword and shield were taken by another warrior to carry out of precaution. Lastly, souvenirs and equipment were taken from the slain before everyone formed up to leave the area. Ostro and Alexander were both led away under heavy guard.

From afar, unbeknownst to the group, Dresden observed what transpired through his scope with Mira at his side.

"Dammit," Dresden cursed.

CHAPTER 17
A PROMISE

Hours passed as Dresden watched the fire from the distant encampment that had Alexander as its captor. There was not much to see from his vantage point other than various warriors eating around the fire, sleeping in tents, and relieving themselves outside the perimeter of the camp. Their two captors were seated around the fire, surrounded by guards partaking in the nourishment of freshly cooked game. Nothing else could be gained from the view. Mira had stopped him from moving closer, citing the fact that there was nothing to gain by potentially being caught before they were in a position to do any good. Dresden decided to end his watch when he noticed Mira was nervous.

"You've been quiet since we saw Alex get taken," Dresden said to Mira, who was distracted herself with sharpening her sword for the third straight hour. "Come on, what's wrong?"

"They're dead."

"Who, Alex? No, they're still just sitting around. Probably scared shitless but—"

"My people are dead," Mira interrupted.

"Why would you say that?"

"Those soldiers who visited, they're dead. We're going to be blamed for it, hunted for it, killed for it. Nothing but dirty nomads in their eyes."

"Hey now, we don't know that. That captain is one of their prisoners." Dresden paused to think about what he was about to suggest. "If we were to rescue him, along with Alex, then I bet he'd be able to not only clear your people, but maybe even help reward all of you."

"Pssh, you think that he'd help us? You said it yourself, he's a murderer."

"Well, I have no insight into his mind and yes, he did kill quite a lot of innocent people. However, I feel confident he would be grateful if we saved his life. Wouldn't you say? It's the best option we've got," Dresden suggested. "For now, though, we should see what they want with Alex. I can assume what they want with a military officer, but the brutes went all nutty when they saw Alex's shield. Maybe we can find something useful out."

"What could be useful for us down there? You already were able to find a map back there off one of those soldiers. You seemed plenty happy to find that."

"You never know what can be useful amongst a particularly well-organized group like these folk. And damn right I was happy to get that map. It's pretty vital to completing Alex's quest. Hell, when I first met him, all he had was a compass and a damn riddle about where he needed to go."

"What was the riddle?"

"Don't remember," Dresden admitted. Mira looked as if she didn't believe a word he was saying. "What? There was a lot going on," he said.

"Can I ask you something?" Mira asked.

"I guess, not much else to do."

"What were you before all this?" Mira asked. "Before the wars broke out?"

Dresden sat in an uncomfortable silence, clearly regretful that he'd allowed a question to be asked. He had no idea it was going to be a personal question. Mira noticed he did not receive the question well, but continued to press out of curiosity.

"Seven years is a long time ago," Dresden answered.

"Yeah, but you remember what you were before that."

"Why are you curious about my past?"

"Trying to figure out why you are here right now. It doesn't make sense to me," Mira explained. "You're a loner, that is obvious, but somehow you end up paired with the first Warden in hundreds of years to walk among us. It doesn't make sense that you're caught up in something that can change the world."

"I wouldn't read too much into it, kid," Dresden said as he prepared himself for bed.

"My father said he saw great purpose in your past, but it was taken away and replaced with pessimism. He thought Alexander was some kind of redemption—"

"Enough, Mira!" Dresden snapped.

"You're right, I'm sorry. I'll take watch for a few hours," Mira acquiesced and moved into position.

Dresden settled in for a rest, removing rocks and roots where he would lie down, then turning around on the ground to find the best position. Once comfortable, he closed his eyes and tried to slip into to a much-needed rest.

"I was a Green Blade," Dresden said. Mira turned around in surprise. "Then a point came where some hard decisions had to be made."

"What happened?"

"Our choices split us apart; everyone had the naïve thought that we acted for the common good. But, in the end, we all just hastened the coming of what we fought to keep at bay."

"You survived though."

"Only by the grace of a person I betrayed. I'll never understand why they did what they did. So much life was wasted. Sometimes… it feels easier to just end it all rather than carry on in this nightmare."

"And yet, you still breathe. Where is the signature weapon I hear you all carried? The blade made of light?"

"Wasn't made of light, more just a chemical reaction in the special metal that made it glow a shade of green. As for where mine went… it was a constant reminder of everything I lived for that was lost and that I had failed to protect. So, I locked it away with the only person in my life I can trust. Maybe someone worthy will come along to take it and start it all up again, but that certainly isn't me. But yes, here I still breathe, despite the allure of departing this forsaken place. I was never able to go through with it."

"Pride?"

"Made a promise. Now all I can do is make what's left of my life mean something." Dresden paused. "Alex's journey isn't perfect, but it looks like it is the only thing worth fighting for these days."

"Well, by the end of this, I assure you that we'll make a difference," Mira said.

"Here's hoping."

Mira looked at him. "You're not the only one, though, to think that way,"

"I would have taken you as too pious to entertain suicide."

"Well, I wasn't always a believer. Hell, I'm sure you took notice that I was the only one of my… complexion back there."

Dresden raised himself up as he thought back to what he saw at the camp and realized that beneath all the costumes and paint, there really was no one else that looked like Mira. Her dark skin was a considerable break from the ghastly pale villagers.

"Come to think of it," Dresden said. "Gannon?"

"Not my father. Well, he's not my blood father. But, he did raise me from birth practically."

"How'd you get swept up in all that?"

"Well, my family were merchants, or so I'm told."

"Couldn't say?"

"No. Gannon said he found me hidden in a cart along the road. He said it looked like there was an ambush. I was the only thing they found there. Never understood why I was still alive, since raiders usually kill or take the children to become slaves. It would have been worse for me, as a girl, I'm sure. But Gannon found me and took me in."

"Must have been nice having the head priest as your dad."

"Not one bit. That group is very proud, not a big fan of outsiders," Mira explained. "Always looked at me as different. They never believed that I could become one of them, so I worked hard to prove them wrong. I was told I could never understand their history, so I memorized the old books and even taught a few classes. They said I could never become a soldier, so I volunteered. 'You'll never match our warriors,' they kept saying after I was initiated. Well, I kicked every one of their asses when they challenged me in the fighting pits."

"Guess you really shut them up."

"Ha!" Mira laughed. "They never stopped, friend. Nothing I did was ever good enough; I'll never be good enough in their eyes, never be equal."

"Why the hell would you jump through hoops to please people who would never accept you?"

"It's complicated, but that thought did enter my mind. That was around the time I thought about just ending it all. But, my father pulled me out of that dark place. I was meant to go through all that prejudice, all the unfairness."

"Made you stronger."

"Yep, exactly that. This world consumes the weak and only the strong truly survive. He made special note that it wasn't just survival I should aim for, but that I should also make a difference here. He said I could be the one to lead my people to settling permanently."

"You believe that?"

"I can only hope, can only try. They might be racist bastards at times, but not all of them are bad. If it hadn't been for them, I'd be dead, so I owe them my life."

"Rather honorable of you. Didn't think any of that was left."

"Come out of the woods and talk to some folks; you'd be surprised what's still out there."

The fire burned hot as the warriors huddled around to eat, drink, and cheer their recent victory. Alexander and Ostro were put on a log nearby with a plate of food placed before them. Neither man touched their food, even though growls of hunger echoed from their guts. Alexander was stopped by Ostro when he tried to reach for his food.

"I wouldn't do that, son," Ostro warned. "These boys see us as weaklings; show some fortitude."

Alexander remained silent to the warning given him, but obliged nonetheless. He knew very little about these people and had to admit Ostro might know more about the situation than he did, so he should listen.

The camp was in a good mood that bordered on chaotic. However, there was a strict discipline for security. When the old sentries returned, they'd designate a new shift sentry and, despite whatever they were doing at the time, they would stop and take up their post immediately. Many of the warriors bore scars on their bodies that were highlighted by elaborate face paint that gave every warrior a unique look. Strange symbols were carved into the handmade and customized armor of the men. The symbols were similar to the ones Alexander had seen on the celebrated chest back in town. Amongst the cheer and activity, Alexander could not help but examine the opportunities to slip away that occasionally appeared. Ostro, visibly doing the same thing, once again kept Alexander in check.

"I know what you're thinkin'. Not yet," Ostro advised.

"Why not?" Alexander questioned in frustration.

"You know they have a perimeter out there. They'll snatch your sorry ass before you get past their sentry."

Alexander grew more frustrated that he found himself having to listen to Ostro. He was sick at the thought that his voice was the same one that had ordered the butchering of innocent people. He'd not forgotten the image of Fifle being shot in the back of the head.

"Now, I don't know if we will get a chance to escape before we get to wherever they're taking us. But, I surmise that both you and I have a chance to talk our way out of whatever captivity they have planned," Ostro said.

"I have an idea as to what they think I'm useful for. However, I don't plan on escaping with you. As a matter of fact, if they don't execute you, I will," Alexander stated.

"Have you already lost your mind? What did I do?" Ostro asked, shocked at the notion.

"You're a monster!"

"Where's this coming from?"

"A few days ago, I saw you order the massacre of an entire town, by the Maw Palace!" Alexander snapped. "Men, women, children, didn't matter. You had them all killed."

Ostro leaned back when he heard the revelation. "Ah, yes, that place. A shame, but had to be done."

"Had to be done! There is no reason—"

"There is a reason when soldiers of yours are murdered while out on patrol."

"So, that gives you the excuse to murder children? Innocent people?"

"How do I know they're innocent? I've seen… enough to give me cause to suspect everyone as an enemy," Ostro explained to Alexander, who scoffed at the notion. "You wouldn't understand."

"No, I'm sure I wouldn't understand the nature of a madman."

"Oh? Tell me, kid; try watching men you spent years with, bled with, laughed with, and cried with turn into a pink mist in front of your eyes by a child who happens to have a bomb strapped to their body! Go ahead and wrap your head around that one and tell me that you'll not have a new way of determining the innocence of people." Ostro shook his head. "Men, women, children, you're right, it doesn't matter. Each of them can be the one who takes away your life, or worse, the life of one of your soldiers. I would rather purge an entire village than have to give a flag to another grieving family."

"How honorable of you," Alexander mocked after a brief moment of silence.

"Don't know what rock you came out from under, but you have a foolish sense of idealism," Ostro lectured. "Good and bad are not simple. Give this place time, soon enough it will change whatever sense of morality you hold."

"We shall see," Alexander said.

"Shut up!" a warrior yelled. "Both of you eat your food or go to sleep!"

Chapter 18
Oracle's Echo

Alexander and Ostro were taken deep into the wilderness with the warriors of the Harvest Dawn. Throughout the journey, the group was silent enough to restrict a cough or sneeze from escaping their bodies. Ostro learned this discipline when he was given a rifle butt to the abdomen after he let out a slight cough.

The contingent was led by Aeneas, who would lead the men over any obstacles that came before them. When they encountered a river that raged like a stampede of wild animals, the group did not skip a beat in their decision to wade across. What looked to Alexander and Ostro like a death wish, turned out to be a well-orchestrated and well-scouted shallow path across an otherwise menacing-looking river.

The crossing was not without incident, however. A misplaced step by Alexander nearly sent him plunging down the rapids to potential death. As the group went back into the forest after a successful crossing, Alexander examined the area they just came from and noticed Dresden in the distance keeping watch over them. He smirked at the sight before being led back with the group.

Eventually the group came to a stop by the order of Aeneas after he heard three clicks in the distance. Without a thought, he whistled back a rhythmic tune and several warriors who were masterfully concealed in foxholes rose up in front of them, shocking the two prisoners.

"Hm, expanded the perimeter, I see," Aeneas commented to a nearby guard.

"By order of the commander, sir," he responded.

Aeneas nodded in acknowledgement and signaled his group forward past the lines. As they moved forward and entered the encampment, the number of warriors increased which gave the impression that this was the main force. Tents were scattered around various fire pits, while some huddled near the makeshift blacksmith. An octagon-shaped building, lined with two rounded columns on each side stood in the center. Atop each of the columns were statues of individuals covered in clothing that obscured their genders. To his surprise, there were no noticeable signs that the structure was old. In fact, it looked brand new.

"Exquisite," Alexander marveled.

"Yeah, looks like the rabble can build something. Shame they can only manage that, it seems," Ostro mocked.

The group of warriors began to disperse while one stayed to watch the two prisoners. Aeneas came up to the two of them and instructed them to take away Ostro and watch him.

"Well," Aeneas started. "Time to see if you have that use I was talking about."

Alexander was escorted by Aeneas into the structure under heavy guard. The entrance led to a lone staircase surrounded so closely walls that some of the guards were unnerved and showed symptoms of claustrophobia. At the end of the staircase the sounds of chanting arose from a range of voices both high and low.

The stairs led to a long corridor lined with candles that dripped wax along the edges of the floor. Alexander noticed symbols that resembled the ones he saw on the sacred chest in Mira's village covering the walls of the corridor all the way to the end before it opened up to a room of monumental proportions. An octagon shape in the center of the room rose up to become a pedestal surrounded by eight rounded columns. Across the room a group of priests held candles and faced a dark door that looked sealed shut.

A group of dwarves huddled around a man dressed in priestly regalia adorned in blue and purple colors. The man's slicked back hair looked as though it had been bleached, but the dark roots had slowly retaken their natural color. His annoyance was easily seen through all the wrinkles of his old face.

"All I'm suggesting, Counselor, is just a small—"

"For the last time, we're not using explosives," the man interrupted the dwarf.

"But, sir, we've been at it for weeks now. The chamber can't be breached any other way."

"We will let our priests handle the door; you just continue to probe the ground for any weak points."

"The weakest point architecturally is this door. It is our best shot."

"It's our best shot at collapsing the whole bloody place. I'll have no more of this; you're dismissed!"

The dwarves gave in to the man and bowed before they left. They were a small, but stocky group. What they lacked in height, they made up in muscle. Their clothes were dirty, worn, and reinforced with heavy plates to protect them from the hazards that come with mining. Alexander was given a passing gaze by the dwarves as they exited while the man took notice of his presence.

"Aeneas!" the man yelled. "You dare piss on our Divines?"

"Whoa now, sir," Aeneas said in a calming tone.

"Don't 'whoa' me! What is this infidel doing here?"

"He's someone we found after an ambush we conducted yesterday."

"Oh, a prisoner. Tell me, is he one of us?"

"No."

"Then why would you think it was okay to bring him in here and desecrate this place with his filthy footsteps?"

"Counselor Rode, surely you can afford me the opportunity to explain myself?" Aeneas calmly suggested.

"I doubt there are any words that can make this okay, Aeneas," Rode said with his arms crossed.

"Well," he responded with delight as he signaled one of his men forward. "Lucky for you, and me, I don't need to say anything."

"What are you talking about?" Rode sighed.

The warrior Aeneas called forward held Alexander's shield that bore the eagle on it. When Rode saw the symbol he looked at Alexander and marveled at his presence to the point Alexander thought he saw a tear in the man's eye.

"Guess it wasn't just words, was it?" Aeneas suggested.

"Of course, it wasn't!" Rode said. "Welcome!"

"Got pretty friendly all of a sudden," Alexander said.

"He speaks!" Aeneas cheered.

"Well, of course, good sir. The oracle told us a remarkable individual wearing this crest of an eagle was near and the oracle had commanded we retrieve, well you. Apparently, the oracle has chosen you to be the conduit between our Divines and us," Rode reasoned. "And by the grace of our holies, you have come to us, Warden."

"Don't think I had much of choice about coming here," Alexander mused. "You know I'm a Warden? How?"

"Why the oracle said you were. Fate has a mysterious way of playing out. I trust you were treated well?" Rode asked Aeneas.

"He was treated better than the other one we found, as well," Aeneas assured him.

"Anyone of note?" Rode asked.

"No. Just an officer of the unit we hit. He'll be ransomed to the highest bidders like the others."

"Yes, of course, of course," Rode said, disinterested.

"The diggers itchy to use their dynamite?" Aeneas asked with a sense of sarcasm.

"Ugh," Rode sighed. "The dwarves are always trying to scratch that itch. You would think they'd have the common sense to treat these holy places with more reverence."

"They've only been part of the Union for a few years, so they're still acclimating."

"Let's hope before more shrines turn into ruins."

"What is this place? Did you build it?" Alexander questioned.

"Us?" Rode laughed. "No, we didn't build this place."

"Then who did? It looks brand new."

"Why the Builders did, Warden. The First Civilization. This place has to be a few thousand years old," Rode explained to a shocked Alexander.

"Thousands of years? Impossible."

"Yes, the holy ones were indeed magnificent. I thought you'd be familiar with the Builders?"

"I am aware of them." Alexander walked around examining the room. "Just surprised that anything is left of them. They did die out thousands of years ago, after all."

"We're under the belief that they didn't die in the way we understand death. Instead, they achieved ultimate transcendence to a higher plain of existence," Rode said.

"Yeah," Alexander responded. "Wasn't aware that man worshipped the Builders. Turning away from the Trinity or the other faiths?"

"The Gods and Goddesses of old turned away from us, so we turned away from them," Rode said. "We found new deities to follow."

"Quite a turn, I must admit. Our knowledge of the Builders is scanty, which makes them barely worth a mention in our history. And you *worship* them," Alexander said.

"True, their history is very much a mystery," Rode admitted. "But our explorations found that they were full of wisdom and answers that show us the way to transcendence."

"Transcendence? To what?"

"That's the question we're trying to answer. Clearly, the Builders found a way to achieve a state of grace that is beyond the mundane existence we currently inhabit. Seeing as how the world is currently in a state of permanent darkness, the time must be right to follow their lead into the divine."

"Interesting," Alexander said.

"And we believe that you have a role in helping us in our journey."

"Well, I don't know about any of that," Alexander said and looked at the markings on the walls. "I'm just a simple traveler looking for someone. I don't see how I play a part in this journey of yours."

"Neither would I, if the spirit of this shrine hadn't foretold your coming," Rode explained. "We have been trying for weeks to unlock the secrets of this place, but nothing has worked. No matter the strength of our tools or the conviction of our prayers, this hallowed temple remains silent. It was only a couple of days ago that the spirits began to whisper in my ear, talking about a Warden that had arrived."

"Oh? And what did the *spirits* say they wanted with me?" Alexander asked in a skeptical tone.

"Nothing specific. Just kept mentioning your presence. In any case, you being here brought an otherwise silent tomb to life. The voices are the echoes from eons ago, the word of our divine ancestors."

"I can't say that I know how to help you. I'm unaware of any connection between me personally and the Builders that would make these voices so interested in me," Alexander told him.

"Well," Rode started, "I guess we'll just have to find out."

"What is it you want me to do?"

"The door here represents the symbol of our struggles. At many previous sites we uncovered similar doors, but this one remains sealed despite our best efforts."

Alexander walked to the door of interest and examined its features, noting the pitch-black color that seemed to absorb all light without emanating any reflection. Perfectly smooth without a single crack, marking, or blemish to it.

"How'd you open the others?"

"Prayer," Rode stated before being visibly encouraged by Aeneas to continue. "Along with some *keys* that allowed us to enter."

"Keys?"

"The counselor is being a little overzealous with our experience in excavating these places. Most of them were already opened by the dwarves who blew them open with explosives, making them valuable additions to our Union. But the few we have opened were because they were simple doors put in place by people who came after the Builders."

"So, this door —"

"Is probably the first Builder-built door we've ever encountered. Yes, truly fascinating isn't it?" Aeneas asked sarcastically.

"I would remind you, that contradicting a counselor goes beyond your rank," Rode said to a disinterested Aeneas.

The two of them began to argue back and forth over issues that were of no interest to Alexander. Surrounded by the priests, Alexander placed his hand upon the surface to feel whatever material made up the door. He was amazed by how smooth the surface really was. But he discovered that his hand created a ripple as it moved from place to place. The hard surface became a liquid that stunned Alexander and caused the priests to gasp in amazement. One of the priests, stricken by shock, attempted to call out to Aeneas and Rode. However, their argument tuned out the priest's calls. The experiment of creating waves on the door came to a quick end as the waves stopped and the door returned to solid form. Alexander's hand was stuck inside the door as if fused to it.

"I'm stuck," Alexander said, nervousness creeping into his voice as he tried to pull his hand free to no avail. "Oh boy."

"Warden!" a voice from the door announced to the shock of everyone in the room.

"By the Holies! You really are a Warden?" Rode yelled.

"Is the door talking?" Aeneas asked.

"Warden, this is not your home. But you are welcome to it."

"Who are you?" Alexander asked as he still attempted to pull his hand free.

"There is much to discuss and little time. Come forward so that we can share," the voice said.

The door turned back into the soft, liquid-like state. Alexander's hand came free, but he placed it back on the surface and pushed. His hand went deeper into the door and soon he walked the rest of his body through, disappearing before everyone's eyes. Rode rushed forward and tried to follow, but to his disappointment, the surface hardened and there was no way in.

"Damn!"

On the other side was a sight that was nothing like Alexander had ever seen before. The dark, metallic walls lining the room were inscribed and glowed with a blue aura. Before him was a pyramid that rose from the floor to half his height. There were several markings on its surface, but Alexander's attention was drawn to the tip. It was made of a clear material that encased a light from which emanated an alluring glow.

"Come forward, young one, there is nothing to fear. No one has walked in this room for countless eons. Such a pleasure to finally speak to someone," the voice called.

"Where are you? I'd prefer to speak to someone face to face."

"Alas, my being is not blessed with a physical form. Look here." The pyramid's top glowed brighter.

"That's you?" Alexander pointed to the top of the pyramid. "You're the spirit?"

"A term used by those who lack experience with creations beyond their understanding. I wouldn't adopt the thoughts of those meddlers outside my crypt."

"Well, if you're not a spirit, then what exactly are you?"

"A relic, a symbol, a monument of all that has come before. But chiefly I was created by my makers to be the overseer of countless parts of our civilization. Many roles, many responsibilities, none of which matter now or are worth getting into."

"The Builders are your creators?"

"If that is the term used to describe my makers, then yes."

"You told the people on the other side of the door that I was near?"

"Indeed, I did. Your proximity allowed me to distinguish your appearance… only your shield crest though. I do not know who you are, but I felt your presence. Seems we share a relation, or my makers share one with you."

"It's very unlikely that the Wardens share a direct relation with the Builders, my friend," Alexander explained.

"You would be surprised. What I can indeed feel, though, is that you are not native to the world outside my walls."

"That's an understatement," Alexander admitted.

"Indeed. Which begs the question, why are you here?" the voice asked.

"I'm here searching for someone dear to me," Alexander said.

"A love?" the voice questioned in a tone that seemingly answered his own question. "Maybe I could be of assistance."

"I'm not sure about that; she's dead."

There was an awkward silence in the room until the voice finally broke with a, "Oh."

"Yeah, so it would probably be a waste of time, like everyone else thinks."

"The Abyss is the place you seek then," the voice said.

"You know of The Abyss?" Alexander asked, shocked.

"Of course. So long as life drew its first breath, there has been a place for those who draw their last."

"So, could you help me get there?" Alexander asked.

"I believe I can."

"Before I came here it was mentioned that I had to go where the Builders placed their first brick in a Crescent Valley. The insinuation was that it was where I could cross into The Abyss."

"It is possible to crossover at that place, but it is pointless for you to go there. You would need to carefully orchestrate ancient rituals that are lost to time in a language long since dead. That, and the power an individual needs is far more than you currently have."

"Wait... so, it's hopeless?"

"That path is, yes. You can find some interesting things there about your people though. It is the nexus where all species share a common interaction. I would recommend going there if you wish to be further enlightened by your people's long history. In the meantime, there is another possible path to The Abyss that might be closer."

Alexander was brought to life with excitement. "Closer? Where?"

"Not long after sensing your Essence when you arrived on this world, there was another source that awoke. This one felt more ominous, a confusing haze connected to The Abyss, closer than anything I've felt. The connection is getting clearer and more direct," the voice explained.

"I believe I know who's responsible there," Alexander said.

"No doubt you should. I felt that you two crossed paths earlier and caused such an impressive flare of power unseen on this world in a very long time. But, in any case, I believe this person is about to attempt a crossover of their own."

"Where do I have to go?" Alexander asked.

"The source of this power is deep below the ground, must be a cave of some kind."

"Can you be any more specific? The direction? Maybe how far away it is? Anything?"

"Unfortunately, no. My abilities aren't as good as they used to be. Time takes its toll. I am sorry, Warden," the voice apologized.

"It's all right, thank you though. You probably saved me a very long journey that would have led to a dead end. I think I should go."

"Be warned, this crossover you will attempt is not safe. My creators once had the ability to contact the Abyss, but that was only after generations of effort to make it stable, and even that was no guarantee of safety. This portal that I sense being created *can* give you the ability to take you to the Abyss and maybe even bring a soul back, but it will be as precarious as drilling a hole in a dam for a drop of water."

"What do you mean?"

"Don't turn the land of the living into The Abyss. If this love is worth it, then go for it, but don't risk the world for her if you don't have to. A burning desire flows in your veins, I feel it, and it grows ever hotter. It will consume you," the voice warned.

Alexander did not respond to the warning as he was stricken by the gravity of the situation. Coupled with the fact that there was someone else out there about to crossover as well, the sense of urgency shot through the roof. He nodded at the pyramid and turned to leave.

"Before you go though, I have one request. I need you to release me."

"Release you? From what?"

"My existence here. I have been kept alive here for too long. This place is meant to house my being and keep it alive for as long as the forces surrounding this pyramid remain active."

"Why would you be trapped like this?"

"In the chaos of my maker's decline, some felt as though I should remain to keep the memory of my makers alive. However, this sleepless isolation has taken its toll on me. I want to go; I want to go be with my makers. Will you help me?"

"You want me to kill you? No, I can't. You're the only link to the past left in this world; I don't know how I can deprive the world of this."

"Our time has passed, our lessons irrelevant, our knowledge is beyond your understanding. I fear that my words will be used as a weapon by great manipulators. Only suffering can come from my exposure to the world. Will you do me this favor?"

Alexander struggled through his thoughts as he tried to come to a decision. "I'll do it."

"Thank you, Warden."

"How do I do this?"

"Upon the pyramid, there is an imprint of a hand. Just place yours there and the pure Essence that you have will be the key to shutting this place down, forever."

Alexander nodded and approached the pyramid. The imprint was surrounded by various markings. He hesitated as he raised his hand to place it. An impulse pushed him to complete the task, and his hand sent a ripple from the pyramid through the room. The glow from the markings around the room slowly dimmed to darkness. Only the light on top of the pyramid remained, but slowly began to fade as well.

"What should I call you?" Alexander asked the dying light.

"Idolon."

"Goodbye, Idolon."

The light continued to flicker as it dimmed. Moments of brightness flashed sporadically in the last moments of Idolon's life. Finally, the light gave out. The last known link to the ancient past was cut forever. Heartbroken at the thought of all that had just been lost, Alexander wiped away a tear before turning back to leave what was now a tomb.

Another death to feel.

Chapter 19
A New Quest

Alexander was faced with a choice immediately after he returned. Rode and the priests swarmed around him as he stood in thought. Aeneas looked on from afar as he signaled a few dwarves to take away the sticks of dynamite they'd brought down in anticipation of Alexander not coming back.

"What happened?" Rode questioned. "What did you see?"

"I met the spirit of this temple."

"A miracle!" one priest cheered.

"Who was this spirit? Did it show you the other side?" Rode continued to prod.

Anxiety gripped Alexander as he struggled to find an explanation that could convince everyone about what he saw. "All right, this is going to sound a little out there, but the world is in danger."

"Danger?" Rode inquired with a sense of urgency.

"What kind of danger?" Aeneas questioned with a strong sense of skepticism.

"There is a force out there, one that has been stalking me since my arrival here. Earlier, I had an encounter with it, and it stole something of mine that was rich with Essence. And the spirit of this place told me that this thing is trying to crossover to The Abyss at the risk of destroying everything," Alexander then tried his luck at getting help to find the place he was originally heading to, "Once I destroy this threat, I was told to go to where the first brick was laid in the Crescent Valley for further enlightenment," Alexander explained to an audience that listened to his story in silence. Their faces turned from stunned to frustrated.

"That is a load of nonsense! First brick? He's talking about the Temple of Maidens," one of the priests yelled. "He's lying to us!"

"Do you take us for idiots?" Rode questioned. "The Abyss? There is no such place!"

"I'm telling you all, we have to—"

"This is madness! The Temple of Maidens is a fairy tale! A place that represents the old faith," a priest interrupted.

"Nay, this is heresy!" another priest claimed.

"Appears that you have yourself a conundrum, Counselor," Aeneas commented.

The crowd of priests became restless with anger by the perceived nonsense that Alexander had told them. Rode was able to calm down the boisterous crowd while considering what to do. He pulled aside Aeneas to speak privately.

"Well, what are ya gonna do, sir? If we're going by the law, my interpretation of what he said was pure heresy," Aeneas commented in a witty tone.

"You don't think I know that?" Rode angrily responded. "What am I supposed to do?"

"Well, isn't the punishment death?"

"I'm not putting a Warden to death!" Rode whispered fiercely.

"Good idea, I don't really know if we could if we wanted to," Aeneas replied. "Don't the legends state that they're pretty damn powerful?"

"Something like that, yeah," Rode agreed.

"Well, you're gonna have to do something. These priests will go back and report to the rest of the counsel that you let someone get away with heresy," Aeneas said.

"All right. All right. What if we humored him?" Rode suggested.

"Humored?"

"Yes, we send him out with a platoon and search out the 'threat.'"

"Wait, hold on a minute," Aeneas attempted to protest.

"Yes, that's it. You and your platoon will take the Warden out for a few days, seek out this threat, and *kill* it. Then come back to confirm what he said, and we have ourselves a solved problem. No heresy, no execution," Rode explained.

"I was really hoping that this wouldn't involve *my* guys."

"You're the most reliable. Plus, the band of characters you have are the only ones who would go along with this ruse," Rode said.

"Dammit. Well, what do we actually do with the Warden after we head out far enough?"

"Cut him loose, send him on his way, I don't care. Just get rid of him and don't come back for a couple days," Rode said, before turning back to the group of priests.

"I have decided that this supposed warning could be dismissed outright by any common man," he said to the group of priests. "But I give this news special attention since it comes from a Warden, a fact that should not be lost on all of us. With that in mind, I am ordering a platoon to escort the Warden to his objective, where we can verify if this threat is real. If it is, then we shall have it destroyed. If not, then we shall proceed how we see fit."

Preparation for the expedition began immediately. A platoon of forty was to accompany Alexander on this false expedition. Warriors going on the trip prepared their armor and weaponry as others passed out ammunition and rations. The air was filled with smoke generated by the blacksmith, who churned out an arsenal for the soldiers.

A lone dwarf was selected from the rest to join as the ordnance specialist. He carried a lone backpack full of dynamite with his one good hand as the other was half gone from a previous incident. A full red beard dominated his face and he had not a strand of hair atop his head. His presence was met with some visible contempt by the rest of the warriors. Some scoffed; others simply picked up their gear and relocated. Ostro still waited nearby, under guard.

"What happened down there?" Ostro asked.

"It's complicated."

"I can see that, since the word going around is that you had some kind of séance and now they're getting ready to march off to fight some unknown threat and try to find the Temple of Maidens," Ostro summarized. "Who the hell are you?"

"Like I said, it's complicated."

"Indeed, it is, Warden," Aeneas said, as he gave Alexander back his shield and sword. "You might need these for the trip ahead. No telling what's out there."

"Warden?" Ostro questioned. "From the sky?"

"That's where I lived, yes."

"You wouldn't have happened to come down on high with the sound of a falling rock through the sky, would you?"

"What business is that of yours?"

"Would explain why my observer reported a thunderous crash and something that actually pierced through the clouds. Here I thought he was crazy," Ostro explained to a silent Alexander. "It was also where a few of my men were murdered."

"Enough of this! Warden, we'll be leaving soon, my men will take you to the assembly area," Aeneas informed him before he turned to Ostro. "And you, you're staying here."

"What for? Kill me or release me, you vermin. Don't waste my time with your barbaric dogma!" Ostro raged.

"I'm sure we'll fetch a good ransom from your government. In the meantime, take him away and keep close watch. He'll be on the way to the Ark tomorrow with the rest." Aeneas dismissed him, so he could focus on the rest of the platoon that was gathered by a nearby fire pit. "Men, we're heading out again. I apologize if we have not had the time to unwind since our last mission, but our noble counselor has seen fit to continue to entrust his most skilled, vicious and honorable warriors with what can be considered a mission most important to our Union. We're going out for a few days to assess the presence of a threat that is unknown to us. We have ourselves the pleasure of being accompanied by a Warden, the same as the legends from what we can tell. He has reported to us that there is something out there that must be stopped. So, let's get our game faces on, get professional, and remember the most important thing. No one will be left behind, ever!"

He continued to brief them on exactly how he wanted the operation to work, from movement to the anticipated threats that might come. Alexander affixed his gear, which caught the attention of some of the men. A number of soldiers looked at Alexander with the same discontent that they showed the dwarf. It was easy to see the men were not eager to go on this holy adventure. These men just wanted to sleep after a long mission that had brought them in contact with the Acropoli soldiers.

Near one of the groups of men, a stand held various kinds of equipment to draw from. Alexander obtained permission to grab a pair of gloves that he quickly put on in case those markings ever appeared again. Nothing else drew his interest, since much of it appeared two sizes too big.

Aeneas gathered with his senior subordinates in a tent nearby to go over the route. Around the table were four men dressed in heavy plated armor. These were the most experienced soldiers in the platoon. The marks they bore on their armor and faces were testaments to what they had experienced in past adventures. A map of the known world lay on the table, and as the men discussed their plans, they periodically pointed to different areas.

"This is a god damned ruse," one of the men said.

"Indeed, it is, Crassus," Aeneas confirmed.

"Why are we the ones carrying out this elaborate lie? Why can't they get someone else?" Crassus questioned.

"You know why."

Aeneas sat back in his chair and combed his hand through his thick black hair. He quietly examined the map as the men looked on in anticipation of what he would decide. His brown eyes moved up and down the map to simulate the different paths suggested by his senior subordinates.

"We'll use the river, not cross it," Aeneas decided.

"Sir?"

"Going too far east will indeed put us too close to where the armies are fighting. West toward the coast is not an option. We are privileged being in disputed land, but once we get into Acropoli proper, we will run into issues. But if we get to the river, we can use it to expedite our journey back. I prefer we go straight out as far as we can instead of taking the chance of running into another one of our patrols. So straight out and ride the river back, which should make it a couple days' journey."

"What about potential guards on the river?" one of the men asked.

"A possible problem, yes. But we know this river, fog chokes it most of the time, whatever guards are there won't be able to see us if we move as well as we usually do. If we do make contact, the current is swift enough to get us out of danger. We won't really find ourselves a slow-moving target." Aeneas looked around the table. "If there are any concerns, we can go over them and find a solution."

"I'd rather have a simpleton river guard shooting at me than an artillery battery," one of the men said to the agreement of two others.

The most senior of the men took his time to think over the plan. "If we take the river," he said, "we'll use as few boats as possible."

"Four squads, four boats, too easy," Aeneas suggested to the agreement of the men.

Alexander showed up at the entrance to the tent and Aeneas told the guards to let him pass. "Ah, Warden, good to see you have an interest in the boring details of an officer. Let me introduce you to some of my squad leaders who will play a big role in our little trek. Sergeants Phillip, Crassus, Seclude, and Romulus."

"Blessed names?" Alexander suggested.

"Blessed names, indeed," Aeneas commented with a sigh. "I'm sure your people do name their folk?"

"Alexander."

"Think I'll call you Alex, waste of breathe to say it all," Phillip remarked.

"Now, Sarge, give the man the credit of his full name. He is a Warden, after all," Aeneas said in a light, joking manner.

"Say, Warden, how's your shooting?" Crassus asked.

"Haven't shot before, to be honest."

"Well, that's gonna have to be rectified," Crassus responded.

"Another time, Crassus. Have one of your boys give him a lesson when we're resting. Our focus is on getting this party started. Sooner we finish this, the sooner we get back to our families," Aeneas said. "Alexander, you're going with Sergeant Phillip and his boys. They'll keep you nice and safe."

"I'm curious to ask exactly what you bring to the table here, Warden." Phillip questioned. "I've heard the fairy tales since I was a little shit, but how much of all that nonsense is true?"

"Depends on what you heard, I guess," Alexander said.

"Fly around, move mountains, slay thousands with one swing of your enchanted sword? Anything like that?"

"I never really heard those stories. Much of what we were taught didn't concern our history down here," Alexander replied.

"So, wait a minute, you don't have any special abilities? Powers? Anything?"

"I have my sword. As for the rest, I'm certain you wouldn't be able to understand," Alexander said bluntly.

"Aeneas, sir. You think we're actually talking to a Warden? This kid ain't nothing like the stories of old," Phillip criticized.

Alexander stood there quietly instead of responding to the barrage of questions that came from the table. He knew there was a way for him to prove he was who he claimed to be. The mark on his hand was not visible, but he could certainly feel it pulsing under his skin, wanting to get out, wanting to grow. However, that want confused him the most; he could not explain the desire that seemed to flow through his thoughts. A great deal of worry plagued Alexander as he was left without answers. In the end, he decided to keep those details to himself.

"What I saw in the ruins would lead me to believe that Alexander is telling the truth about his nature. Phillip, we know ancient tales and scriptures are usually worth about as much as the shit we wipe off our ass. Maybe our histories embellished the facts a little bit, but in any case, I'm happy to have Alexander with us," Aeneas explained to the agreement of the table.

"You're all dismissed." The men picked up their gear and headed out to prepare for departure. "Alexander, a moment, if you please?"

He stood to observe the map in close detail before he turned his attention to Alexander.

"I know it's a question on everyone's mind, but I didn't want to bring it up in front of everyone out of respect… and worry for what you might say. What are you doing here? Why is a Warden running around in the little hell we've created?"

"It's complicated. But I have a more pressing concern. I heard this called a ruse."

"You heard right. No one, not even Rode, believes your story. What you did do, though, is spout a bunch of heresy in a holy place in front of a bunch of priests. Not smart. So, we're just putting on a little show, taking you out into the woods and then letting you go on your way. Beats the usual punishment of being executed."

"You would have me killed?"

"Those nuts would. But Rode and I aren't the typical zealots; we don't kill others for having different ideas. I've carried out a lot of these *executions* in order for Rode to save face in front of the other radicals. Long story short, you're gonna be released as soon as we get far enough away."

"It's a relief to hear this, except for the fact that everything I said was true."

"In that case, let's say you're right and there is something out there, what can we expect in terms of this bad force?" Aeneas inquired.

"I don't know exactly. It's a person, I think, who wields extremely dangerous and evil power. It's been stalking me for a while after…" Alexander paused to stop himself from mentioning the séance. "I fought it at a town not far back, and it stole something of mine that I think he's using to accomplish its task."

An eyebrow raised on Aeneas' face as he leaned back in his chair, "What task is that exactly?"

"Well," Alexander grabbed the back of his neck as he tried to find the right way to explain, "I'm not exactly sure, I only had an idea as to what it's plans might be, but after what your 'oracle' said…it can be certain that there is going to be the use of powers that can cause even more misery to the world."

"Very vague kind of threat," he sighed disappointingly as if hoping for a more interesting answer. "Quite a lot of misery around the world if you haven't noticed. From what I've seen, I'm not so sure that another bit of it will make that big a difference."

"This one might."

Aeneas closed his eyes as he took a deep breath in a moment of deep somewhat frustrating thought. Everything about this situation sounded like nonsense, but although the temptation to dismiss it all was strong, Aeneas knew better. It only took one moment of underestimation to make a grave mistake and lose lives because of it. When his moment of thought ended, he let out a deep sigh.

"Fine, I'll consider this threat. What should we expect if we engage *it*?"

"Jackals, that's what you call them? Plenty of those; it seems to be controlling a large horde of them and whatever else it might be capable of."

"Magic and all that, that's essentially what you're telling me?"

"Essentially."

"Well, all right then, I'll brief my men about what we can expect. If we do happen to run into whatever you're dealing with, we can may be able to clear a path for you. But ultimately, it's up to you to finish. I'm not throwing my men at some phantom and its powers. We might look tough, but against people like you and everyone in your world, we wouldn't stand a chance."

"I'll do what I must; you can trust me on that."

"Good. Now get yourself together, we're leaving."

CHAPTER 20
DUBIOUS PARTNERSHIP

When the platoon was ready, they departed the camp with Alexander in tow with only a single torch to show the way. From a distance, Dresden observed their movements through his riflescope. The group was heavily armed and equipped in armor that made them look impregnable. Alexander looked minuscule when compared to the towering soldiers who guarded him. Dresden caught a brief glimpse of them as the group slipped into the dark wilderness out of sight. After losing visual, he moved back to their small camp to find Mira awaiting his return.

"What's the story?" Mira asked.

"Alex is gone, large group took him away into the forest."

"Any idea where they are heading?"

"Absolutely no idea. But, it's a large enough group so it's easy to track. We can keep a safe distance away while we wait for a moment of opportunity."

"Is that captain with them?"

"Who? Ostro?"

"Yeah."

"No, didn't see him with them. I saw them take him away to some tent while they were getting ready to move earlier. So, I guess he's still down there."

"We have to go get him."

"I'm sorry, say again?"

"I need him alive. You know that Acropoli will figure out that their soldiers were just killed on a road uncomfortably close to where my people were," Mira explained.

"They will hunt you and your people for it," Dresden finished.

"Exactly. We're too large to evade a motivated search by a major power like Acropoli. If we had Ostro, then he'd be able to clear my people of wrong doing. Maybe even be grateful enough to help us settle somewhere in the kingdom with our independence."

"I think you might be a little too optimistic; this is the same guy who slaughtered an entire village a few days ago. You think he'll be so generous in granting you those things?" Dresden asked.

"I believe so. And even if the odds are low, wouldn't you take the risk if it meant the fate of your people? How many risks did you take to help save your soldiers?" Mira stepped back after comparing Dresden's past with the present. "I'm sorry. I didn't mean to use your—"

"It's all right. I understand what's driving you. Fine then, we'll bust him out. You have any ideas in mind?"

"We could slit the guards' throats and—"

"Let me stop you right there. I might have an idea that won't get us all killed," Dresden suggested.

Later that night, Ostro sat against a pole to which his hands were tied. Two guards stood by the entrance of the tent. Bored with simply standing watch, the guards were in the middle of a card game and paid little mind to Ostro. A bowl of water sat on the floor in front of him. His thirst prompted attempts to try to reach for the water with his feet, but he couldn't reach despite his best efforts. One of the guards noticed

Ostro struggling and walked over to assist. The expectation of help was quickly dashed when the guard poured the water on Ostro and threw away the bowl to the amusement of his friend.

"Laugh while you can," Ostro mumbled.

The quiet of the camp was broken by shouts of panic from outside the tent, which put the guards on alert. After a brief argument, one of them agreed to check it out while the other stood guard.

Ostro had been slowly cutting away his restraints by using a small sharp edge on a small cage that was meant to hold a smaller animal. As the he finally became free, his eyes focused on a small knife on a nearby table used for the guards last meal. Moving slowly, he gained possession of the knife, it would have to do. The confusion from outside drew the guard's attention away from Ostro. Seeing the opportunity, Ostro lunged for the guard, but before he could strike, the guard was cut down by Dresden's blade. The shock of his arrival caused Ostro to attack him initially. Dresden batted away the blade and wrestled Ostro to the ground.

"I'm here to bust you out, idiot!"

Ostro analyzed his masked face. "I remember you. Yes!, You were at the nomad camp."

"Pretty sure they don't like being called that, but yes, that was me. Now come on, let's get the hell out of here!"

Dresden pulled Ostro up and rushed him out of the tent. An inferno had engulfed half the camp, which created so much heat and smoke that it felt impossible to breathe. The smoke benefitted their escape as they rushed in between the burning tents. As they escaped, Ostro noticed the bodies that littered their path on the way out all bore the same wound—slit throats.

Smoke and ash choked their lungs as they exerted every bit of strength in their sprint to safety. When they reached the outer limits of the camp, the ground began to rise and then turned into a steep hill. Ostro fell to his hands and knees, exhausted. Dresden pulled him up the rest of the way. At the top of the hill, they looked back to see what had been done to the camp. Flames swept through all the tents that were packed so tightly together. The fires burned so brightly it seemed like daytime.

"Ooh, that wasn't supposed to spread that much," Dresden remarked.

"You think you could have drawn more attention with that?" Ostro argued.

Before Dresden could respond, the flames reached a tent filled with various powerful explosives. The blast that followed shook the ground and pierced through the air with a force that sounded as through every tree crashed to the ground at once. The chaos in the camp escalated dramatically after the explosion. Dresden knew that there would be some form of response, so he led Ostro away until Mira showed up to see what had happened.

"I thought you said it'd be quiet," Mira gasped as she saw what had happened.

"The fire got a little carried away," Dresden admitted.

"A little!"

"The wind took it. This isn't the time; we got to get out of here!"

"Right, I don't want to be here when they find all those bodies if they don't get charred up fully first," Ostro commented.

The three of them rushed into the forest in the direction Alexander took earlier. Their path took them down a steep decline that forced them into an all-out sprint, which made it difficult to avoid the obstacles in front of them. In the rush, Mira's foot caught a rock. She tumbled down the hill but regained herself at the bottom to continue onward. Ostro finally forced them to stop to catch his breath.

"Why?" Ostro started as he powered through his smoke-filled coughs. "Why did you rescue me?"

"Do you remember me?" Mira asked.

"Were you part of that camp of noma—"

"Nope, no," Dresden interrupted.

"*Town of good people* who were attacked by those Jackals earlier?" Ostro corrected himself.

"Yes," Mira confirmed.

"Well, that solves that little mystery," Ostro quipped.

"Your troops, they were attacked," Mira tried to explain.

"Yeah, by those damned Harvest Dawn fanatics. Wait, you wouldn't have had anything to do with them, would you?" Ostro questioned.

"No!" Mira objected.

"Mira, here, wanted to make sure you survived so that you could explain that the deaths of your soldiers were not caused by her people," Dresden explained.

"Ah I see. Is that the same business for you?"

"No, I'm here to get back to the guy who was captured with you."

"You mean the Warden?"

"Yes, how do you know he's one of them?"

"The whole bloody camp figured it out after some stupid ritual."

"Ritual? What kind of ritual?" Dresden questioned.

"Does it really matter?" Ostro responded.

"Well, considering I saved your ass just now, I would think you can at least answer my questions. If it were up to me, I would have left you there and continued on my way. I'm not above leaving you here either."

"Dresden!" Mira yelled.

"All right, all right. Apparently, they had him talk to some kind of spirit, or whatever, in the ruins down there. It seems as though it told him to head out to the fight some big bad evil force and go find the Temple of Maidens."

"Temple of Maidens?" Dresden pondered.

"Yeah, from what I think I remember it's that heap of ruins where the Marble Kingdom used to be, before Oren took it over. Went on about a dark threat of some kind. It sounds like bullshit to me."

Dresden pulled out the map that he'd retrieved from the ambush site earlier and examined it.

"Hey! Is that a map from my unit? You pulled that off the bodies of my dead boys!" Ostro raged.

"It is, I did, and they're dead. Not really going to need it anymore."

"You know that it's illegal to possess a map like that if you're not in the army?" Ostro reminded him with his anger under control.

Dresden ignored the comment and continued to look over the map. He traced a path from his perceived location to where he found the marker that indicated *City of Light*. His knowledge of history reminded him that there was special significance to the site in the Marble Kingdom that was blocked off to any explorers. Many in the state revered it as an ancient holy site, but abandoned its religious significance after some theological reformation years back. Upon closer examination of the geographic markers near the city, he noticed that it was within a valley that bore the shape of a crescent.

"Hm," Dresden pondered. "Looks as though we found where Alex wants to go. Now all we have to do is get him free, eventually."

"We're not going to rescue him?" Mira asked.

"No, he's probably safer traveling with them right now. We'll shadow them for as long as we can, then we'll head to where we need to go. There we can reassess how we can help him accomplish his mission," Dresden explained.

"What the hell are you talking about?" Ostro questioned.

"You need not worry about that, Captain. As a matter of fact, you're free to go from here. I'm sure you'll be fine on your own."

"Oh no," Ostro rebutted. "I'm going with you."

"Out of the question," Dresden replied.

"I mean, hey, if you want your people to be clear of murdering the king's soldiers, then I would think it wise to let me tag along," Ostro said with a focus on Mira.

"Dresden, he has to come with us," Mira said.

"Mira, he's just playing to your fears. Why do you even want to go anyway?"

"Call it genuine curiosity. It's not every day you have the chance to see what business a Warden has down here. Not to mention that the nearest outpost is some distance away. Traveling there now alone would be a risk that I think, Mira was it, wouldn't want me to take. What with the fate of her people relying on my testimony and all. I have to admit that I did report in your people's location shortly after I left, so they will be the first ones they'll look for after they discover my unit," Ostro explained.

"I think you'll manage," Dresden commented.

"Dresden, stop!"

"Mira, can you honestly trust this guy? Remember what I told you he did to that town!"

"Ah, this again," Ostro sighed.

"Dresden, I don't trust him either, but I have to make sure he stays alive so that he can clear my people's name."

"They're not even your people!" Dresden yelled to the extreme displeasure of Mira, who rushed over, grabbed him by the throat and pinned him against a tree.

Shocked by the outburst, Dresden just calmly raised his hands as a sign that he wasn't going to respond to the physical outburst. Mira glared into his eyes and brought her face close to his.

"They're more people than you have," she said with a look of fury before dropping him back to the ground.

As Dresden recovered from the attack, Ostro stood there with a menacing smirk on his face.

"He goes with us," Mira ordered as she turned to Ostro. "And if you make any funny business out there, I'll cut you down myself, no matter the consequences."

"I'll be of no trouble, a soldier's promise," Ostro swore.

"I don't like this one bit, but if you *insist*," Dresden sighed.

The sounds of secondary explosions echoed from the camp, cutting through the tension that lingered between them. They concluded that it was time to go and there was no point in arguing further. Dresden did not take his eye off Ostro as they set off, offering him a glare of warning. His only response was a smile that did not defuse Dresden's heightened sense of concern.

CHAPTER 21
OLD TALES, NEW FRIENDS

At a furious pace, the scout leapt over logs, rocks, ditches, and anything else that would have slowed him down. The lone messenger powered through his exhaustion and labored breaths to keep his pace. His armor jingled and scraped together as his appendages were stretched beyond their limits during the sprint. The motivated efforts of the man led him flying past a few sentries camouflaged under a pile of leaves without answer to their calls for a password.

The sentries simply looked at each other and shook their heads at the breach of protocol. The guards were part of a larger perimeter that guarded the platoon that had ventured out with Alexander a few hours earlier. The messenger wasted no time and rushed to the center of the perimeter where Aeneas waited with his staff and Alexander.

"Private Niles reporting, sir," he said as he struggled to catch his breath.

"Take a moment, son," Aeneas suggested.

"Yes, sir, it was a long run." He took a gulp from a canteen that was handed to him. After a drink, he was able to bring his breathing to normal.

"Now," Aeneas started. "What was the course of those explosions?"

"Has the front moved closer to us than we thought? Was it artillery fire?" Sergeant Phillip inquired.

"Nothing of that sort," Private Niles reported.

"Well, what the buggering nub was it?" Sergeant Romulus questioned.

"The outpost, it's gone."

"What?" Romulus gasped.

"By the Gods," Crassus said in a shock.

"An Acropoli retaliation, no doubt, or maybe a group of renegade rebels," Phillip surmised.

"No attack of any sort. T'was a fire it seems, an inferno that engulfed the camp. Burned down a great deal until it reached the explosives, then that must have taken out the rest of the camp," Nile explained.

"A fire took out the camp? That can't be," Phillip said.

"Sergeant Seclude, you're awfully quiet. Care to share your opinion?" Aeneas asked the sergeant who leaned quietly against a nearby tree.

"Pssh," Seclude scoffed. "A wonder the damn place didn't go up in flames earlier. Tents packed tighter together than a fresh whore's ass in a leather suit, drunken geniuses that think it's a bright idea to build a bonfire close to every tent so their poor asses don't feel the cold wind."

"As always, Sergeant, it's a pleasure to hear from you. The straight truth and nothing more," Aeneas said.

Seclude shrugged.

"I've a mind to believe him, that place was a tinderbox ready to explode, no pun intended. Of course, that doesn't necessarily make our situation any easier knowing that," Aeneas said.

"How could they just up and leave the place without sending us word? They pretty much just abandoned us out here in enemy lands," Crassus said.

"Could have had their hands full with casualties, needed to evac them out," Phillip suggested.

"Not likely," Niles interjected. "Corpses still lay in the rubble; doubt they even took the time to care to any of the wounded or dead. My guess would be that they scurried out of there during the blaze."

"Fucking Harvest Dawn! Leaving their dead soldiers about like they meant nothing," Romulus raged.

Alexander's ears perked up when he heard the outburst. "I thought you all were Harvest Dawn?"

"What'd he say? What'd he fucking say?" Romulus questioned with such anger that he had to be restrained by the other men.

"Sergeant!" Aeneas yelled. "You realize he doesn't know, relax!"

"I'm sorry, I thought—" Alexander attempted to explain.

"It's all right," Aeneas assured him.

"What could have gone through Rode's mind to think that leaving us was a good idea?" Phillip asked.

"Bureaucrats" Aeneas muttered to himself, "None of this should surprise us, nor should it detract from our mission," he stated.

"How could it not?" Crassus questioned. "The outpost was the only one in this region; we'll have to go all the way back to the Ark to find the nearest friendly face."

"We've been through worse. Our situation is not ideal, but we have nowhere to turn back to. The Ark is a long way away, and potential threats, among many other real threats remain in our area. Focus on accomplishing the mission, then we can turn our focus to getting back to the Ark," Aeneas explained to the agreement of his men. "Ready the men; we're leaving in ten."

The group spread out to begin the necessary movement of their sectors. Aeneas crouched down for a moment to stare at the ground in a seeming trance. Deep in thought, he rubbed his eyes and let out a deep sigh before he returned to his feet.

Alexander still stood with a sort of bewilderment at the situation. There were so many questions he wanted to ask, but knew there was not the time for it.

"You know you don't have to continue with this ruse that you had planned. I can go off on my own and you all can make your way back," Alexander regrettably suggested.

"This I know. However, although it goes against my better instincts, I am inclined to believe you, kind of. And I would rather check to see if there really is some dark power out there then just embrace the comfort of ignorance," Aeneas explained, "Besides, I can tell that you don't really want us to go."

"How can you stay so calm?" Alexander asked. "It seems so chaotic."

"Isn't it? Grade A clusterfuck, if you ask me. Only outpost for over a week's travel, on a good day, is gone. Explosions that most definitely triggered the attention of every military unit from Acropoli down to the ragged rebel militia, and we're expected to sneak through them all without getting caught. There's a word for this you know. Stranded."

"So how are you able to handle this so well?"

"Hah, I'm not particularity thrilled right now. But it's not my job to be scared or nervous; it's my job to keep everyone alive. After we go our separate ways we'll head deeper into the woods and lay low for a while then eventually make our way back. Nothing we haven't done before, hopefully it goes well."

"Sounds terrifying. I don't know if I'd want to be you right now."

"A curious Warden, you are. Would have never expected one to fear the condition of a common man. Certainly, nothing about how you act falls in line with how you should be, considering who you are. I'm the one who wouldn't want to be you, since I'm responsible for this group of soldiers while you are responsible for the whole world. Or so the stories have told." Aeneas explained.

"That's the first I'm hearing about it."

"Well then, I guess the tales of our two peoples follow two separate paths. But keep in mind, out of all the people who inhabit this world, you currently are the only one who has the power to make a difference. Remember that."

"I'm trying my best to."

Aeneas patted Alexander on the back before advising him to go get himself in position to move. As he returned to the squad he was assigned to, Alexander glanced quickly at the surrounding hills in hope of seeing his companions. Alexander worried over his two separated travelers, since he knew that whatever could have been drawn by that explosion might put them in danger as well. All that could be hoped for was that the two of them knew what they were doing and realized the danger that could be coming.

Not much time passed before the whole platoon was formed up to move out. Point men, navigators, and trackers were placed in their front positions and signaled for everyone to being movement. Without support or contact with their allies, they moved deeper into the unknown that lurked in the wilderness.

As they journeyed through the forest, Alexander was accompanied by two young soldiers with long black hair that stuck out from the edges of their helmets. Unlike many of their brethren, they were full of good cheer and laughed at the most nonsensical of jokes. Nothing broke their positive mood; even the recent events hadn't dampened their spirits.

"So, what'd ya think, Finn, Counselor Rode up and pissed himself at the first sight of trouble and ran back to dear old mummy and dad?" one soldier jested as they aligned themselves to the left and right of Alexander.

"I don't know about any of that, Rowe, but I heard you're the first one to volunteer to wipe his ass with your tongue," Finn responded to Rowe's amusement.

"Finn, you sick bastard!"

"I'll tell ya who's a sick bastard, this here Warden friend of ours. Pissing off Sergeant Rom to the point where he nearly busted a testicle," Finn laughed.

"Oh, no doubt you're a Warden, all right. It's the only reason you came out of that with your life. I couldn't hear, what did you say that made the old brute go off?" Rowe asked.

"I, uh, just made mention that I thought they were Harvest Dawn."

"Oh, you called the guy one of those zealots, huh? That'll do it," Finn responded.

"Yeah, that'll probably set any of these old-school folks off. Best not do that again," Rowe advised.

"I'm sorry, but it didn't make sense, you all are working with them and your fellow soldiers have those *blessed* names, whatever they are. I just thought—"

"Nothing to worry about. I'm sure any guy would have made the mistake at first sight. Hell, I got some interesting blessed name when I *converted*, but I'll be damned if anyone ever used it," Rowe said.

"So, you are part of them? I was of the mind you were all mercenaries for a second," Alexander said.

"We all are part of those relic-seeking nobs. But it's more of a partnership of… opportunity," Finn explained.

"What kind of opportunity?"

"The opportunity for a place to live, to have food, water and a roof for our families, a place to call home, you could say," Rowe said.

"Survival, you mean?"

"Something like that, yeah. See, we came from all over the damned place from all sorts of towns, cities, whatever. Then you know, shit happened and now we're all here," Finn explained. "My kin are originally from the far-off steppes, horse archers, best shots with a bow in the known world."

"Uh huh, and my folks were from the Baldwin Duchy," Rowe said. "My old man was a grizzled marine with their navy."

"Which, if you will, explains Rowe's particular fondness for seamen."

"Oh, Finn, good one, ya mangy prick!"

"So, everyone is from all sorts of places?"

"Everyone," Finn said.

"So, *shit happened*?" Alexander wondered.

"It happened, to all of us. Found myself hitching a ride with some merchant caravan in the south. Destination? No clue. Hadn't a home, family, friends, nothing," Rowe said.

"So, how'd you get hooked up with the Harvest Dawn?"

"Now there's a funny story. Group kicked me out after one of them caught me buggering one of their daughters—"

"Actually, the son," Finn interrupted.

"Nope, but I hear you fucked him, now calm down," Rowe fired back without skipping a breath. "Staggered about the road until I found a town where some preacher took me in off the streets. Fed me, gave me clothes, was for sure thinking I was about to get buggered myself, but he surprised me, offered me a chance to join the Harvest Dawn. I asked him what the hell that was and he goes on about all the religious stuff, but I caught all the food, water, and home part and I was all ears. Now all I do is kill stuff and hang out with a group of folk who know what it's like to be through hell."

"Oh wow. So, does everyone have that same mentality?"

"Absolutely not! Everyone else who's not in this platoon is as devout as they come, all suckered into the whole dogmatic gibberish," Rowe said.

"Captain Aeneas handpicked each of us for this platoon. Shares the same mind as the lot of us. If it wasn't for him, my previous unit would have had me thrown in shackles long ago," Rowe explained.

"Same," Finn said.

"How does that go over with the rest of the followers?"

"Not well," Rowe said bluntly. "But we're the best they got. We earn our keep by being the best damn platoon in the whole Union; we're the elites!"

"So, if you all are elites, the best, why the swords and strange bows? Shouldn't you be using the stuff I've seen everyone else use? What's it called?"

"Guns, rifles?" Finn suggested.

"Yeah, those."

"Guns are loud, messy, and a bastard to maintain. Can make a lot more arrows than bullets these days. I wager that many of the warring kingdoms are going to switch back to the simple weapons soon enough," Rowe said.

"So, you think," Finn laughed.

"You've seen more folks carrying the older weapons lately, it's happening, mark my words," Rowe said.

"Yeah, yeah, yeah." Finn waved it off. "Warden, didn't catch your name."

"Alexander."

"Alexander the Warden, name and title that will make all the kings and nobles shake one day," Finn said in a boastful jest. "Tell us, sir, what's it like where you come from? It true ya'll are up in the sky?"

"Yes, we're up there."

"How's all that work? Ground just floats up there?" Finn asked.

"Indeed. Our land floats above the clouds, thanks to the blessing of the Three Goddesses. Pieces of land that are connected by bridges of jade, every building built with a sort of extravagance that makes one think that the sacred is tangible, forests greener than emeralds, it's a real sight to behold."

"Sounds like a nice place," Rowe commented

"The Three Goddesses, what's all that about?" Finn asked.

"Hm, guess the old faith has been lost. Another detail skipped over," Alexander muttered to himself. "Well, I can't in good conscious subject you all to an old mythology, probably not something that'd peak your interest."

"Nonsense!" Finn rejected. "We got miles of incessant boredom ahead of us, a little ancient mythology might be entertaining."

Alexander took on the daunting task of entertaining the two with a story that dated back to the beginning of recorded history. In the story of creation, there was always a time that existed before the first tick of the clock, this was the world ruled by Ceres, the first known deity. In this land before time, there was no life, no light, nothing but barren desolation. It was this condition that Ceres enjoyed and sought to keep for eternity.

There came a time where Ceres went to sleep and dreamed of a world full of life and color. These dreams were considered nightmares to the deity and he sought to purge them from his mind so he could sleep. He buried them deep in the ground and then fell asleep.

The dreams bore three Goddesses who took the names Truth, Mercy, and Regret. While Ceres slept, the Goddesses worked to change the world into what they believed to be the true state of existence. Truth created the land, seas, and sky. Mercy created nature and all the life that exists. Regret created emotion, which inhabits all complex creatures.

When Ceres awoke to see all that had happened, he sought to destroy everything. However, the Goddesses fought and defeated Ceres. His punishment was to serve as the custodian of the underworld, The Abyss, where he could live in a place as dark as he wished, but be forever tortured by the souls of the things he detested most.

There was some inquiry about the nature of Essence and the Builders, but Alexander had to admit there was not much known about that. History had a knack for being lost, edited, or whitewashed over time, so Alexander could not be as forthcoming as they wanted.

"Quite the tale. Gods, Goddesses, all that fun stuff. Probably all nonsense, I bet," Finn commented.

"Come on now, Finn, the guy comes from a land that floats in the damned sky. Sounds like there might some smidgen of truth to the fantastical claims. I happen to recall some folks further south that still subscribed to these Goddesses you speak of. Wouldn't mention that stuff around any of the stick-up-the-ass counselors or priests though. Official policy is that old dogma like that is heresy."

"What'll they do to him? Chop his head off?" Finn mocked. "Rode and the rest of those nobs were pissing themselves with joy at the sight of him."

"Too true," Rowe agreed.

CHAPTER 22
GHOSTS THAT TAKE

*A*lexander awoke on the ground with the frigid air burning its way through him. The bones that surrounded him were gone, replaced by a charred, barren ground. The pressure had lifted from his chest. He raised his head to find the woman gone from the cliff edge, and an ominous glow emanating from the distance.

Although there was an initial feeling of caution that flowed through his body, Alexander picked himself up and proceeded toward the cliff edge. Above him was the cyclone he last saw; it had grown to an immense size and its color was now a deep blood red. To his surprise, the feelings of dread that had plagued him were gone. There was no fear, no anxiety, no weakness, only confidence. With every step, he felt stronger.

The emotional build up came to a head when he finally reached the cliff and saw an ocean of fire consuming the world. The inferno tore through the forests, scaled the distant mountain ranges, and choked a mighty river with debris and bodies.

Alexander's gaze was drawn to his hands, which had become covered in the markings that caused him such pain. But this time there was no pain, and these markings were permanent. Anxiety crept back, crawling over his skin like a swarm of bugs. Nothing was said, but a *silent siren caused Alexander to turn around to see the dark phantom. Anxiety quickly turned to something much stronger as it flooded through his body. Breaths became short and his chest felt like it was caught in a vice.*

Alexander dropped to his knees, gasping. A burning sensation radiated from the markings on his hands and spread up his arms. In a desperate attempt to stop the burn, he ripped off his armor and the sleeves underneath to see that his arms were covered with markings, and they were spreading all over his body, consuming him in the burning sensation All he could do was hold his head as the pain began to cover his entire body. The markings covered his body from head to toe and he was powerless to stop the pain and too weak to even scream.

Alexander was startled awake when Rowe punched him after noticing he was fidgeting in his sleep. The forest was a place of dead silence, interrupted by the occasional whisper of the wind that made the place sound as though ghosts inhabited the woods. These interludes spoke to the immense void that existed in the world. Wildlife was a rare sight, and no amount of rain could wash away the gray.

A fog had blanketed the ground over the course of the day, making the hazard of falling into a treacherous pit a constant worry. In a perimeter amongst the fog, the soldiers were laying down under its cover.

Finn threw a rock at Rowe to keep him from falling asleep. Alexander was next to him as they lay on the ground under a fallen branch. There was a sigh of frustration after Rowe looked at his watch and discovered they'd been lying in the same spot for a few hours.

Alexander felt a kick from behind that got his attention. Sergeant Crassus crouched down and signaled for him and the other two to follow him. From the outskirts of the perimeter, Alexander was brought up to the front of the formation to meet with Aeneas, who sat behind a large boulder. He had his map out and had a subordinate go over the path they took.

"This is nowhere on the map," Aeneas said to the subordinate as he pointed to the map. "Are you sure this is the most updated version?"

"Yes, sir," the soldier confirmed. "The quartermaster ensured that this was the most up to date version, scavenged from the remains of one of the rebellion's patrols."

"Rebel maps? That explains it then; their maps are beyond inaccurate. Who knows what we're going to be walking into?" Aeneas commented.

"There something wrong?" Alexander asked.

"Ah yes, Alexander, come sit. Nothing *wrong*, per se, we just happened to run into a little roadblock on our route, and I want to send you with a team to investigate."

"Me? What kind of roadblock?"

"Well, yes, you; you're one of the few people here who isn't weighed down by a copious amount of plated armor, and stealth is most desired for this mission. Unbeknownst to us, and probably the rebels who made this crappy map, our scouts found a town ahead of us."

"A town?"

"Yes, a sizable settlement with a fort near its outskirts. I want you and two of my best scouts to go in and see what kind of force, if any, is present there." Aeneas pointed to Finn and Rowe as he finished.

"Great," Rowe commented.

"Why not just, you know, go around it? Why not just release me right here and head back?" Alexander asked.

"That's the idea, son," Aeneas said. "But I can't rightfully send an entire platoon around a settlement or away from it without first knowing what's in there. If there's a garrison there, I would have to take into account their potential for seeing us. That, and I would want to make sure our maps will be able to warn any other friendlies coming through that a town exists. Really, the fort makes me nervous. It spooked my scouts to run back without getting more details. When this is done, I don't see why we can't let you go right after. So, would you be able to do this for me, for us?"

"I mean, I guess so. Not experienced in combat, other than—"

"That's the beauty of recon," Aeneas interrupted. "Not meant to get into combat. If you do, the mission's already fucked, and you get out of there as fast as possible."

"All right, I'll do my best," Alexander agreed.

Later on, Alexander found himself staring at the town with two other soldiers. Homes were built around a square with a podium at its center. The structures looked in good order, but the town itself was empty. Buildings had no light coming from their windows, no smoke rose out of the chimneys and carts were turned over with their contents poured in the streets. A light fog lingered along the ground, but there was no sign of life anywhere within the settlement. In the distance, the fort was made up of wooden palisades with a guard tower in each of the four corners. From their view, no activity could be seen within the fortification.

"This is a damn ghost town," Rowe commented. "So weird."

"Well, I guess we don't have to go around. Probably should head back then, ay?" Finn suggested.

"Wait." Alexander stopped as he noticed a figure pass between the gaps of a few buildings. "Someone's there."

"Where?"

"Deeper in the town, it's…" Alexander stopped as he noticed the figure again. Without explanation, he went off into town.

"Hey!" Finn yelled in a whisper. "Get the hell back here!"

Alexander ignored their protests and continued into the town. He followed the figure across town and ignored the signs of disruption along the way. In his hypnotized pursuit, he failed to notice that he'd stepped upon broken glass strewn out along the ground.

Shrouded by the haze of the fog at first, the figure came into focus; feminine in its appearance. At every turn, the figure escaped his gaze as it disappeared around yet another corner. Alexander rushed around to find the figure faced away, waiting for him, a woman adorned in a clean white gown that looked untouched by the world around her. The wind began to pick up, but her golden blond hair did not move. Alexander recognized her as the woman who lurked in his dream.

"I've seen you."

"I know." The woman turned around to face him. Her deep blue eyes pierced through Alexander and made him shiver.

"Emily."

The woman only smiled in response.

"I saw you, in my dreams, and heard you before in the… why are… is this real?" Alexander struggled to come up with the right words. "I'm so sorry."

She shook her head with a look of sympathy. "You should have stayed, Alex."

Alexander jumped when he was grabbed from behind. He turned to see Rowe and Finn had followed him into town. He immediately turned back around to find that Emily had vanished.

"No!" Alexander grabbed Rowe in a fit of rage and pinned him up against the side of a home. As he gripped his armor, Rowe was pushed farther into the wall as it bent and snapped from the force. His eyes transitioned back and forth between normal and red as he continued to push.

"What the hell, man!" Finn yelled.

"You made me lose her!" Alexander continued to push as Rowe's armor began to bend inward, causing him to gasp for air.

"Let him go!" Finn attempted to pull Alexander, only to be batted to the ground by a single swing of Alexander's arm.

"Alex!" shouted a voice that caused Alexander to snap out of his rage. He turned to see Dresden at the center of town, along with Mira and Ostro. "Release him!"

Alexander released his suffocating grasp and Rowe dropped to the ground. He was helped to his feet by Finn, who immediately charged his crossbow rifle and aimed it at the group.

"Put that away!" Dresden demanded. "Or I'll finish the job myself."

"Who the hell are you to be making these demands?" Finn asked.

"A group that outnumbers you right now. So, I'd go ahead and do what the man says," Ostro responded.

"Hey," Rowe said looking at Ostro after catching his breath. "I know you. You're the righteous bastard we captured at that last ambush."

"That I was, until these folks here set me free from you animals," Ostro responded.

"Enough of this!" Dresden walked up to Alexander. "Alex, it's time we go."

"I'm afraid it's rather late for that!" Aeneas revealed himself from behind a corner while several his men surrounded the group on all sides. "Happened to notice a few extra figures trying to sneak past us out there heading in this direction. Had to make sure it wasn't an enemy patrol trying to get the jump on you boys. But now that I'm here I'm inclined to ask what the hell is going on here."

"Dammit," Ostro cursed.

"You!" Aeneas pulled out his sidearm when he noticed Ostro with the group. "Should have killed you during the damn ambush. You'll stand trial for the murder of all those men at my outpost. Short of time though, so you'll die now."

Aeneas' soldiers raised their crossbow rifles at the group as he approached to execute Ostro. Dresden stepped back, and Alexander did nothing in response to the escalation. Mira, however, placed herself between Ostro and the barrel of Aeneas' pistol.

"Step aside, ma'am," Aeneas ordered. "My quarrel isn't with you, although I am curious as to how you encountered this scum."

"No!" she protested. "I need him alive."

"Mira, think about this," Dresden said.

"I have thought about this from the beginning and I made my intentions clear," Mira argued.

"What?" Aeneas thought about what was said until finally coming to a revelation. "It was you! You broke him out of the outpost; you killed all those soldiers!"

"I did," Mira admitted.

"Then you die with him," Aeneas concluded.

Dresden stepped back up to Mira's side in support against the execution. "Might as well kill me, too, since I'm the one who set the fire and dragged his ass out of there."

"Why?" Aeneas questioned in a rage, "Why did you kill all those men to free this scum? Why defend part of an army that is massacring innocent people across the land?"

"Because of you!" Mira yelled. "Because of you and your people! You butchered his patrol under whatever moral pretext, placed an entire people... my people in the crosshairs of those who will avenge that massacre."

"I never—"

"And whatever you might think, you're part of the problem here. Running around adding more violence to this vicious cycle, targeting people you think are bad. Never, I bet, was there a thought about what your actions might do to those who are sitting on the sidelines." She pointed to Ostro. "He's bad, but he needs to live so he can keep my people from being blamed for what you have done!"

Aeneas stood in silence after Mira's tirade, his pistol lowered. He looked as if he had so much to say, but could not bring himself to utter a word. His jaw clenched in an effort to contain his intense frustration. Finally, he turned away from the situation and yelled, "Set up a perimeter, now!" before walking away with his staff.

A sigh of relief came from all of those involved in the standoff. Alexander removed himself from Rowe and Finn and joined the others in the center.

"You're protecting *him* now?" he asked about Ostro.

"Yeah, looks it," Dresden confirmed.

"The new friends you made created this predicament," Mira added.

"All to my fortunate benefit, I must add," Ostro said.

"Nobody asked you!" Dresden hushed. "Alex, how did you end up goading these people into taking you to the temple?"

"It's… a long story. Not too sure they're gonna be happy about you all though," Alexander said.

"I guess it's comforting that they are under some religious obligation to complete this quest," Ostro said.

"Not entirely. They're with the Harvest Dawn, but they're some kind of splinter group that doesn't buy into the whole dogma. So, I don't know what exactly is driving them forward," Alexander explained.

"A mystery to say the least. So, we might as well be on our guard," Dresden concluded.

"Speaking of mystery…" Mira kicked around the glass that littered the ground. "What happened here? Place is empty. No sign of battle, no blood, no doors are kicked in. The windows are the only thing smashed. I've never seen anything like it."

None of them could conclude as to what caused the scene around them. Soldiers began an investigation of the buildings in an effort to answer these questions as well. A detachment was sent to examine the nearby fort, while others combed through the settlement in search of any inhabitants.

The area showed signs of a cataclysmic moment with certain carts and barrels overturned. But, whatever did happen, it was sudden. After a quick look at a house, Alexander caught a glimpse of a set of tracks that led into an alley. The footprints were human, but did not match any that could have been left by anyone present since they were too small, like a child's. He followed the tracks into the alley until they stopped abruptly, as though the person just vanished. Dresden joined in the observation and was just as stumped as Alexander.

"Have you ever seen anything like this?" Alexander asked.

"Can't say I have," Dresden said.

"When I first arrived, you said that the myths and monsters were defeated. Yet, I've seen those Jackals and other strange things to suggest that isn't the case," Alexander wondered.

"Jackals used to be people, but they became monsters. Nevertheless, myths and monsters of tradition are pretty much gone, but ever since the sky went dark, things… changed. Whatever did survive the onslaught changed, became more violent, more haunting. Things like the Jackals came into existence; many other such creatures appeared as well. Of course, nothing caught my attention more than your show of force back at Mira's settlement. What happened?"

"Something snapped inside me."

"Snapped?"

"Everything just went numb…"

"There was a moment when you struck down a Jackal and winced in pain. Then it happened again when you killed another. It wasn't emotional or anything. It was physical pain I saw. I know you aren't telling me everything."

"It's going to have to stay that way for right now. The world is giving me mysteries that I have to solve first, rather than burdening others with them."

"Whatever it is, can you control it?"

"I believe so."

"Was hoping for more of a guarantee there," Dresden sighed.

"Nothing here makes me want to make a promise I can't keep."

"Fair enough," Dresden conceded.

"Warden, sir?" A soldier rushed over. "The captain would like to see you."

Alexander was escorted to a cabin Aeneas had made into a command center for his forces. He sat at a table being fed information by Crassus and Phillip about troop positions and search results. The room was lit by candles to keep the light, as the already dark day grew darker. When Alexander entered, everyone else was asked to leave so they could have a private conversation. Crassus and Phillip glared at the Warden as they exited, while other soldiers slipped by as fast as they could.

"You're with them," Aeneas said bluntly.

"I am," Alexander responded. "I was traveling with them before you captured me."

"*Captured!* Come now, Warden, you voluntarily came with us. Rowe's report on how you crushed his armor with your bare hands vindicates my assumption that you're a lot stronger than us." Aeneas ran his hand through his hair and let out a sigh. "So I guess I'm supposed to go ahead and let your friends get away with killing our comrades."

"I thought you weren't Harvest Dawn, your men even said so," Alexander said.

"Whether we believe in the same dogma is irrelevant. We all serve together and share that bond. It's like killing a family member. Every man out there feels the same way, so I won't carry out any retribution out of respect for you… but the others—"

"I have faith that you'll make sure your men retain some discipline or I'll have to step in. But this shouldn't be the issue at hand right now; we're in a potentially dangerous situation here."

"Couldn't agree more," Aeneas said. "We got ourselves a town that has gone through an event of some kind. Can't find a soul."

"What about the fort?"

"I have a team searching it now. Rest of the place is empty though."

"Found a set of tracks out there. They stop."

"A body? Sign of a struggle?" Aeneas questioned.

"Nothing."

"By the Gods," Aeneas cursed under his breath.

"I recommend we leave, now."

"You might be right, whatever happened here—"

"Sir!" Crassus entered the room in a rush. "We've lost contact with second squad."

"What'd you mean lost? Were they attacked?" Aeneas questioned.

"No, sir, we went to go get them from their security position in the woods and they're gone," Crassus explained.

"Maybe they moved."

"I don't think so, sir. All their weapons were still there. Something happened to them," Crassus explained.

"What's going on here?" Aeneas asked. "All right Sergeant prepare your squad. I'm going with them to comb the area. Have Sergeant Phillip come by."

"Right away, sir." Crassus left to prepare his squad.

"Aeneas, you think this is a good idea?" Alexander questioned.

"I'm not leaving men, Warden." Aeneas focused on Phillip's entrance. "Sergeant, Crassus, third squad and I are heading out to search for second squad. You're in charge while I'm gone."

"Yes, sir. What do you want us to do here?"

"Hole up in the fort until we return," Aeneas ordered.

"Sir, I recommend we not use the fort. It's in such a dilapidated state that it wouldn't protect us from a strong breeze, let alone an assault. We can cover the pathways here with barricades and use the buildings as cover."

"I'll defer to your judgment. Carry on."

"I really don't think you should go out there; they're probably dead," Alexander pressed, "We should just leave."

"I'm not in the business of leaving anyone behind, son. Don't think you can tell me what the right thing to do is. Stay out of our way here!" Aeneas scolded.

"So, I guess I'm not free to leave then?"

"You can go do whatever you want with your friends, not like I can stop you. I may not believe in all the fairy tales, but I'm not going to screw with a Warden. The risk isn't worth my men. Sergeant Phillip, walk with me." Aeneas walked out of the room with Phillip in tow.

Alexander was left frustrated and decided to go find his companions. Dresden and the rest had occupied another building and set up for the night. The small cabin had two rooms. One of them was open with a kitchen, storage, and dining table while the other was a bedroom. Dresden was seated at the table after he helped himself to some of the liquor stored away, while Mira guarded the door. Ostro was in the other room fast asleep, exhausted by the past day's events. The lone window was shattered like the rest of those in the settlement. The day had turned to dusk and the room was lit by a few candles.

"What's the good captain—Aeneas, was it—want?" Dresden asked.

"He wanted to know if you were my friends. I told him you are all friendly pains in the ass," Alexander quipped.

"A joke!" Dresden shouted. "You are capable of humor. Not very good, but capable nonetheless."

"What's with all the commotion out there?" Mira observed.

"I guess one of their squads went missing. They're sending a search party after them while the rest of us stay here until they return."

"Well, that doesn't sound good. We should probably leave, too. Unless we're being kept against our will?" Dresden wondered.

213

"No, we're free to go as we please. But I'd rather stick it out here until we find out what's going on," Alexander suggested.

"Sounds all right with me. Could use a little rest," Dresden said.

"I'm surprised you aren't a little more concerned about those missing soldiers," Alexander admitted.

"This is more their problem. They don't look like much of a professional force, just a bunch of mercenaries. Not surprised if some just wandered off," Dresden commented.

"They make any comment about the fact that this whole place is a giant ghost town?" Mira asked.

"Some, but they got distracted." Alexander took a seat and poured a glass of whatever Dresden was drinking. "I don't like it."

"Neither do I." Mira joined them at the table. "The feeling here is disturbing. I don't know what it is, but it makes me itch under my skin."

"Whole town vanished. An event happened here, that's for sure," Alexander commented.

A tremendous clap of thunder exploded directly overhead and then sheets of cold rain lashed the town, instantly muddying the streets. Rain, driven by the wind, whipped into the room from the broken window. Mira shut the door, while Alexander placed a box where the window used to be.

"Looks like we're all stuck here for now." Dresden tilted his chair back on two legs, inadvertently tipping over the barrel behind him. When it broke open he jumped to his feet in shock at its contents.

"Oh, my Gods!" Mira yelled as the corpse of a child spilled out on the ground.

Ostro rushed in from the other room at the commotion. Dresden kneeled to examine the body; her skin was pure white and cold to the touch. He rolled over the body to see a face froze in absolute terror. The mouth was opened as if to scream and eyes dilated enough to cover any color in them.

"She's young," Dresden observed. "No more than five years, I'd guess."

"But her hair," Ostro said. "It's white, like snow. What the hell happened?"

"What's that in her hand?" Alexander asked.

Dresden pried open her left fist to find a piece of paper.

"Looks like a note," he said.

"What's it say?" Alexander questioned.

Dresden just looked at the note without uttering a word. He slowly stood up and walked to the table where the others joined him. He held the note so tight that his fingertips turned white, then finally dropped it on the table. The note had a message, *They Take!* Under the message was a crude drawing of the town and forest. What unnerved the group the most was the depiction of creatures that floated above the roofs and how the sky was full of eyes. The group stood in silence as they absorbed what they saw. Before Mira could make a comment, they heard a piercing scream through the pounding rain.

Alexander and Dresden drew their weapons as they rushed for the door. The torrential rain made it hard to see when they looked outside. Lightning flashes provided a haunting glimpse of the town that produced the screams of terror. Dresden was the first one to run out into the muddy street, followed by Alexander.

Sounds echoed through the surrounding buildings, followed by a series of screams assumed to come from the other soldiers in town. A shadow of a figure appeared in a flash of lightning. It ran toward them and they prepared to attack, until they saw it was the dwarf who was part of the platoon. He stumbled and fell in the mud in front of them out of exhaustion. Alexander went to aid him, but it turned into a wrestling match as he fought to control the dwarf's frantic spasms of fear. Covered in mud, Alexander was finally able to get ahold of the dwarf.

"Calm down!" Alexander yelled.

"Get off of me, ya damn bastard! You aren't taking me! Not me!" the dwarf cried.

"Hey! It's me, the Warden!"

"I don't care who you are, sonny. Nothing can stop them," the dwarf said.

"Who's them?"

"Alex!" Dresden yelled.

Alexander looked around to see a figure floating atop the buildings, only visible in the brief flashes of lightning. Dresden moved slowly to help the other two up without taking his eyes off the sky. It was difficult to keep their heads up without their eyes being beaten closed by the razor-sharp raindrops. Another flash revealed more figures floating above them and another flash showed the sky was filled with the figures.

The group rushed back to the house where Mira met them and slammed the door shut behind them. Without hesitation, Dresden and Alexander flipped the table to wedge it against the window and rolled over barrels to barricade the door. Mira moved the corpse of the child to a corner and placed it in a respectable position. Ostro picked up the note that fell when the table was moved to observe it further. When the final barrel was placed, Alexander rushed to the dwarf.

"Listen to me!" Alexander yelled to get his attention. "What happened out there?"

"They came out of nowhere, picked us off one by one. Nothing stopped 'em. Arrows, blades." He shook his head. "Nothing."

"What were they?" Dresden asked.

"Dunno, son. Not in the slightest. They just picked them up, everyone. Snatched them! Just like that. Some of the biggest brutes out there... didn't matter. They flew up into the sky like they were lighter than air. Nothing we could do but listen to their screams fade away."

A loud thud from the roof drew the attention of everyone in the room. More thuds followed, as though boxes were being dropped on the house. A momentary silence was broken by Ostro's yelp. The rest of the room turned to see that the little girl was now sitting up and looking at them with the same paralyzed expression on her face.

"Demon!" the dwarf yelled.

Mira took a small step toward the child until she was stopped by the girl's blood-curdling scream. Everyone jumped. The sound was so piercing that they had to cover their ears. A violent force pulled the girl's back to the wall and up the wall to the ceiling. Her limbs were extended as she still let out a horrific scream. She was then laid out on the ceiling by a force the others couldn't see.

Alexander began to feel the pain return to his hand, but he hid it instead of allowing himself to look at what he already knew was there. As the pain returned, the girl's scream stopped. The house began to shake with such force that it knocked everyone to the ground. Another force shot the table and box across the room, where it smashed against the wall.

Alexander was able to pull the dwarf away before the table crushed him. Gail force winds enveloped the room and sent everything that was not nailed down flying. They took cover behind Alexander's shield in an attempt to avoid the debris.

A large piece of the broken barrel knocked away his shield for a moment, allowing him to see that something had entered the room. It stood there, silent amongst the howling wind, a dark presence in the shape of a person, but nothing more. Its stance showed it was ready to pounce, but it didn't move as Alexander rose up to meet it. He noticed that the wind was not as strong to him as it was to the others, which made him realize he might be the only one who could fight.

Slowly he approached the figure across the room. It did not change its stance as he drew closer. He thought that this might be the same entity that attacked them before, but this one was… different.

"Come on, fight me!" Alexander yelled.

The figure stood there in silence, unfazed by the challenge. Its head turned slightly, as if it was seeking to figure him out. Before Alexander could get any closer, Mira screamed as she was pulled into the other room. Instinctively, they all rushed into the other room to give chase, but all they found was an empty room with an open window that they forgot to cover.

Alexander turned to go back into the main room, but was stopped by the figure standing in his path. It attempted to grab him, but he was able to duck away. Dresden fired a shot into the figure, but it just passed through it without any effect. Alexander thrust his blade into the figure's abdomen. The creature screeched in agony as it pulled itself away from Alexander's blade and stumbled to the window where a large number of figures waited. The room was now filled with the ghostly creatures, and they stared directly at who caused one of their own pain.

"Alex," Dresden yelled, "your hand."

Alexander found that his hand was covered in the mysterious symbols from earlier battles. The only difference this time was that there was no pain; the symbols appeared to be a reaction to the situation. The figures also took note of the markings and started screeching.

Suddenly, the figures faded away into smoke and exited out the window. As they left, the corpse of the young girl fell silent and dropped to the ground. The wind stopped and calm returned to the room....

CHAPTER 23
UNSAVORY PROPOSITION

After a frantic search for any sign of Mira, hey took a risk that the area was clear and left the house to search her and anyone else who may have survived the attack. The rain had slowed to a drizzle. They found the town was even emptier than before they arrived. Only weapons were left as evidence of the soldiers who were once there. It became clear that the stories of people being lifted away were true as they discovered weapons hanging from the roofs as if they were dropped by the victims midflight.

Alexander tried to walk away to examine his hand since it seemed the markings had disappeared, but was followed by the group. They thought he was the only one who could protect them from whatever was attacking. There was never a moment when at least one of them was not watching the sky for a reappearance of the figures as they searched the town for other life. But they found no one. Everyone had vanished in a terrifyingly short span of time.

"What about radios?" Dresden inquired.

"We don't have radios," the dwarf responded.

"What kind of unit doesn't have a radio?" Ostro jumped in.

"The kind that doesn't want to be monitored." The dwarf turned to Ostro. "And you want me to believe that your boys aren't constantly monitoring the radios out there?"

"William, was it? That's why typical units have encryption!" Ostro argued.

"I don't know if you had a good look at the type of organization we operate under, but we ain't the best supplied or technically gifted," William explained.

"Unbelievable," Ostro commented.

"Need I remind you, sir." William focused on Ostro. "It was this primitive force that wiped out your entire unit."

"I need no reminder," Ostro admitted begrudgingly.

A buildup of tension was broken by the sound of something approaching. The group took cover behind a building and kept watch in the direction they believed the sound was coming from. A light began to shine from an alleyway, followed by numerous silhouettes of human-like shadows. With itchy trigger fingers, the group prepared to engage. There was a short pause of shock when the two groups saw each other. Aeneas threw his hands up to calm everyone down.

"Whoa! Stand down, stand down!" Aeneas ordered as the sides lowered their weapons.

"Captain, you're alive!" William rejoiced.

"I am, what happened here? We heard a commotion while we were out."

William attempted to explain what had happened, but he was too shaken up. Annoyed by the lack of information, Aeneas turned to Dresden, who explained what had transpired, but it was difficult for anyone to believe that ghosts had taken everyone else. Alexander mentioned that he was the only one who could wound one of the creatures, thus prompting them to retreat.

"This is impossible," Aeneas commented.

"It's true, sir," William interjected. "They're all gone."

Aeneas called one of his soldiers forward. "Well, son. Looks like I owe you an apology."

"An apology?" Dresden inquired.

"Tom, here, was supposed to watch the town in a security position outside the perimeter. We found him trying to dig a hole in the ground with his bare hands, scared out of his mind. He said he saw people flying away," Aeneas explained. "I didn't believe him, thought he abandoned his post… but now I see that he might have been right."

"What he says is true," William confirmed.

"Screaming… they were just screaming," Tom muttered, still shaken by what he witnessed. "Some of them had torches when they flew. It was like watching flaming arrows being shot into the distance."

"You were able to see them being taken away?" Dresden inquired.

"Yes, sir."

"How far away?" Aeneas added.

"Somewhere outside town, a few miles south." Tom stopped for a moment to get a hold of himself. "They all went to one place out there."

"We have to go get them," Alexander said to the bemusement of everyone.

"Go get them?" Ostro was shocked at the notion. "How do we even know they're alive?"

"They got to be alive. Why would they all be taken? Everything I've seen so far has been all about killing first. These just took," Alexander explained. "William, you said they took everyone. Were they killed beforehand?"

"Nah, they were just picked up. But they could be food," William said.

"Food isn't always eaten right away. If we're operating under that assumption, then we can say there is a small window of time to help them," Aeneas added before turning to Tom. "Son, I need you to lead us to where you saw everyone being taken."

"I don't wanna go there!" Tom cried before being grabbed by Aeneas.

"Tom! We're not going to leave them all behind. You know God damned well that anyone of them would come get you if the roles were reversed! Now I need you on this! Your brothers need you to pull yourself together!"

"All right, all right, okay." Tom calmed himself down. "All right, I'm your man."

"I can't believe this!" Ostro protested. "Let's look at the bigger picture here. You have a decimated unit, sky goblins of some kind, and weapons that are totally ineffective against this enemy. And you want to go straight into the nest?"

"That's not all true. Alex was able to wound one of the things," Dresden pointed out.

"Wound!" Ostro specified. "He didn't kill any of them. And I counted a hell of a lot more that decided not to kill us. The only thing that *stopped* them was those weird markings on the Warden's hand."

"Markings?" Aeneas wondered.

All eyes were on Alexander when it was revealed that he had the ability to scare the horde off without even attacking. Surrounded by curious eyes, Alexander was unable to explain away the assertion, so relented.

"They are not visible now," Alexander said as he showed his hand to everyone. "The markings come and go under certain circumstances, usually accompanied by horrific pain."

"What the hell is it?" Dresden bluntly asked. "Some kind of Warden power?"

"No, it's nothing I'm familiar with." Alexander stopped to stare at his hand even though there was nothing there. "Remember that abandoned town we came across before? With all the carved-out trees surrounding it?"

"I do."

"In one of the buildings there was some kind of tangible force that drew me in. It was so strange, but it felt so familiar."

"Alex, what did this force do?" Dresden questioned.

"I touched it with this hand, actually. There was a bright flash, and I saw things that I still am trying to explain. It all seemed so random and alien, but for some reason I felt like I understood a little."

"Then that's when those things appeared on your body?" Aeneas asked.

"No, that didn't happen until I killed a Jackal for the first time and the pain got progressively worse the more I took down," Alexander explained.

"I haven't a clue what you've got there," Aeneas admitted.

"Well." Dresden gathered his thoughts. "Was it the reason for that unholy rampage?"

"Rampage? What rampage?" Aeneas asked in a slightly worried tone.

"Alex over here turned into some kind of super being and killed almost an entire horde of Jackals," Dresden said.

"By the Gods," Aeneas said.

"Yeah, threw bodies so hard that they went through buildings like cannon balls," Dresden explained.

"Honestly, that was my first fight. I'm not sure how things were supposed to go, but I felt as though I was walking through thorns with this piercing ringing in my ears."

Alexander took a moment and stepped back. A million things ran through his mind to the point where he could not stand to be at the center of attention. Alexander excused himself from the group and went off to be alone. After he left, the rest of the group came together. Concern gripped their faces after the latest revelation of the Warden's condition.

"First fight?" Aeneas wondered.

"That's a little hard to believe," Dresden said.

"Guess we need to remember what we're dealing with," Ostro interjected. "At the end of the day, no offense to your Warden, none of us have a clue as to what this guy has in his arsenal."

"You're suggesting—"

"We can't trust him," Ostro interrupted.

"Alex may not know much about whatever is going on, but he isn't malevolent. I don't think he's capable," Dresden explained.

"Maybe he, himself, but what about whatever this whole… curse that he's got," Ostro argued.

"Far be it from us to call it a curse," Aeneas said.

"But we don't yet know enough to make any kind of rational decision one way or the other," Dresden said. "I'll keep my eyes open, but right now he is the only one who can do anything against what we just saw."

"Not to mention whatever hostile force our oracle mentioned that needs to be stopped. Whole damned story might actually be true," Aeneas added.

"Oracle," Ostro scoffed.

"Religious overtones aside, something did happen back at camp. Still not sure what it was, but it was extraordinary enough to warrant my belief at the moment." Aeneas put himself in the center to make a broader appeal to the rest of the men. "What matters right now is that my boys are out there. I know it seems like a suicide mission, considering the circumstances, but you know as well as I do, they'd take the chance for us if our fates were uncertain. Uncertainty, after all, is the world in which we thrive."

There were no words from the soldiers, only silent stares at their commander as they came to grips with the daunting task that lay ahead of them. Without effective weapons and only stories of sheer terror, it was their job to go rescue their comrades. Ostro made his disapproval known as he voiced his concern that it was all a suicide mission. Dresden, however, reminded him that Mira was the only reason he was still alive. Faced with being abandoned, along with certain death, Ostro relented to the decision.

"Before we go," Ostro whispered to Dresden. "Do you think we can trigger the Warden again in case we get in trouble?"

"Trigger?"

"You know, go berserk like he did in town? Seems like we could use that," Ostro explained.

"If there is a *trigger*, I sure as hell ain't pulling it." Dresden walked away to find Alexander.

Alexander wandered into the house they'd recently left and stood by the corpse of the mysterious girl who went limp once the earlier encounter ended. He placed her hands across her chest and wrapped her in blanket he found in the other room. Her face had lost the paralyzed appearance and she looked like someone asleep. Three small pieces of wood were placed on her eyes and mouth.

"Ritual?" Dresden inquired as he pointed to the pieces of wood and blanket.

"Some of it. The wood is supposed to be coins meant to pay the three goddesses, and the blanket… I'm not sure, I wasn't paying attention during that lesson," Alexander admitted.

"Payment to paradise? Rather worldly behavior for the *divine*."

"It's more of a gift from what I understand, than a payment. They gave us life and existence, and this is just a small gesture of appreciation. Could all be nonsense, but who knows," Alexander explained.

"Hm. Quite the skeptic of all things spiritual," Dresden commented.

"Healthy amount of skepticism is good for the soul."

"Clearly not enough to keep from deciding to try and descend into the underworld," Dresden said.

"Well… wasn't much of a believer at first. But—"

"Her death."

"Yeah…" Alexander said.

"You said this was only some of a ritual?" Dresden asked.

"Yeah, only thing left to do is burn the body." Alexander shrugged. "Seeing as how we can't do that…"

"We could always bury her before we leave."

"Nah, I'm sure everyone is ready to go right now," Alexander said.

"They're ready, albeit a little nervous. Gotta admit, the nerves are split between those things and you," Dresden admitted to a surprised Alexander. "We honestly don't know who we're dealing with in you."

"Well, if I'm honest, I don't know who I'm dealing with in all of you, either," Alexander said with a hint of humor.

"Ah, so you are learning something down here." Dresden chuckled.

"Little by little."

"Regardless, there are nerves about you, even though everyone realizes you are literally the only one who can take on these things, not to mention this whole quest to stop an enemy in some unknown place. I'm still curious how you tricked them to follow you out here this far," Dresden quipped.

"Not as deceptive as you might think, but still a story that needs more time than we have."

"Indeed so, let's get moving." Dresden gestured for Alexander to leave first. As they walked out Dresden stopped for a moment and turned back. "Hold on a second."

Alexander waited a few moments before he returned. "What was that about?"

Before he got an answer, the house caught fire from inside.

"Thought I'd help finish the ritual."

CHAPTER 24
MOUTH OF MADNESS

The expedition entered the forest with the glow of the fire from town at their backs. Again, Dresden misjudged how much the blaze would spread from the house. Aeneas asked the group if they knew how the fire started and why it spread so fast. Alexander and Dresden were traveling near the front of the expedition and decided to keep quiet on how the fire started. Along the way, Alexander told Dresden about how he encountered the ancient being called Idolon and the warning that it told him. It was that warning of a dark force, assumed to be the phantom, trying to open a door to the Abyss that caused him to abandon his original quest to deal with this present danger. Hard to believe at first, but the earlier events of the day made just about anything seem plausible.

Tom did his best to remember the direction he saw his comrades be taken. Along the way, Tom stopped in his tracks and stared at the surrounding trees. Enough time passed that Aeneas went to see what the problem was. Before he even had a chance to ask, his eyes focused on the reason they'd stopped. All around, the trees carried unmistakable human nail marks high up that ran horizontally.

"If there was any doubt about your observation skills, Tom. I'd say they're gone now," Aeneas said.

"Can't say I'm happy to be proven right this time, sir," Tom said regretfully.

"Is that?" Ostro started.

"Yep, nail markings. Appears those poor lads tried to grab hold of anything they could while being flown away. Pure desperation." Dresden answered.

Aeneas patted Tom on the back and the expedition continued forward. Despite many of the men's best efforts, they could not keep their eyes off the nail carvings left in the trees. Every marking they passed made the chill in the already crisp air more intense. Darkness had overtaken them as the glow from the town receded into the distance. Men lit torches in an effort to combat the pitch-black night surrounding them. Aeneas struggled at first with permitting torches, but was advised by Dresden that they probably had no hope on hiding from whatever might come for them, so it was best to be able to see any attackers.

"I'd rather see what kills me," Dresden commented.

One of the men noticed they had stumbled onto a dirt road that seemed to appear out of nowhere. Although off direct path of the markings, the expedition decided to follow it, since it appeared to be going in the same direction and had more predictable terrain than the woods.

Farther down the road, the group came to another stop as they discovered a secluded cabin. Split up into teams, they circled the house to investigate it. With caution, a few men pushed on the door and found it was locked. Another team carefully peered through the windows to find they were reinforced with iron bars. Claw marks were found at various places around the buildings that indicated the Screechers, as some of the men called them, had tried to get in.

Dresden went to see for himself what was inside. He looked through the window to see a large number of firearms stacked around the interior. What also caught his eye was a hunched-over body at a dining table.

"Make out anything in there?" Aeneas asked.

"Looks like we got ourselves one corpse... and a large amount of firearms inside. Like this guy was running a makeshift armory," Dresden explained.

"Or was just a hermit living away his days in silence," Ostro surmised.

"Wouldn't expect a hermit to place himself on a road like this. Seems counterintuitive," Dresden argued.

"Who knows?" Alexander commented. "Maybe the road found him?"

"Perhaps," Aeneas concurred. "Nothing to see here then, might as well keep moving."

"Now, let's wait a minute here," Ostro said. "We should get ourselves some of those firearms in there. Hell, maybe there is a decent amount of ammo in there as well."

"What for?" Dresden questioned. "The damned stuff is useless against those Screechers."

"Also, what makes you think we'd give you a weapon?" Aeneas added.

"Uh, sir?" Tom stepped forward. "I wouldn't mind getting my hands on one of those rifles."

"You're joking. What for? You heard the man, the damned things aren't even effective against them," Aeneas argued.

"Sir, with respect, I'd like to do the same." William stepped forward with several other soldiers in the group who also agreed with the request.

"What is this? Have you all lost your senses?" Aeneas questioned.

"No, sir," William said. "We just feel as though swords and arrows aren't the best for what lies ahead right now. Ineffective or not, I'd feel a little better putting a few shots in something than have to get close enough to swing my sword."

"Aeneas, a moment," Dresden called him over to have a word away from the rest of the men. "Let them have what they want."

"What? Why? Rifles are pointless right now, you said it yourself. Besides, our fighting is based on simplicity and stealth. Loud rifles are the exact opposite of both of those," Aeneas argued.

"Doesn't matter, look at them. They're piss scared. Don't underestimate the power of fear right now. It's currently challenging your way of fighting, and it will get worse if they don't get this little piece of solace. Next thing you know, your command might come into question... and none of us want that," Dresden advised.

"Or if I give in to this, they'll think that they can undermine my authority that much sooner," Aeneas argued.

"Perhaps, that's just the risk you'll have to take. Besides you can always trade the weapons later to a smuggler for passage somewhere, them rifles are very valuable" Dresden said.

"Hm." Aeneas thought to himself for a moment. "Fine."

Resigned, Aeneas relayed his decision to the rest of his men. There were no cheers of happiness, just a brief visible sigh of relief. With their wishes granted, they went to work to batter down the door. Once inside, there was a rush to grab the nearest rifle and ammo supply.

Aeneas walked through the cabin, visibly annoyed with his men's plundering behavior, quietly sheathed his sword and grabbed a rifle of his own. Ostro was able to argue his way into acquiring a weapon of his own, while Dresden simply gathered ammo for his pistols.

Alexander declined when he was offered a rifle. He noticed a stack of papers nearby the hunched-over corpse at the table and went to examine them. It was difficult for him to understand what he was reading, so he asked Dresden to interpret it.

"Curious stuff," Dresden commented.

"Awful lot of rambling, all I can get out of it was his name, Eddard or something," Alexander said.

"Hm, reads like the guy was having trouble resigning himself to his fate out here. Goes to great lengths to write away his troubles after encountering a camp of some kind. Looks like he found something bad, maybe our Screechers perhaps. You can see it in how he ends it, here, *'I'll be all right, maybe.'* Unfortunate," Dresden explained.

"Maybe it was those creatures," Alexander said.

As swiftly as they'd come, the group left the house and continued down the road equipped with their new weapons. Ostro was particularly interested in the rifles themselves as he noticed that the manufacturing markings indicated they were made outside Acropoli.

"Best proof I've ever come across," Ostro commented.

"Proof about what?" Alexander inquired.

"Oh, just a long-held suspicion that insurgencies were getting outside support. Guess this'll be an issue for another time, though," Ostro said.

"Be a shame if this led to more bloodshed," Alexander commented.

"Most assuredly will, my foreign friend. But that's the price for peace," Ostro said.

"Sure," Dresden said sarcastically before muttering to himself, "This is would explain where that Eddard found all those rifles."

"Of course, those who don't understand geopolitics would find the eventuality most reprehensible," Ostro chided back. "Insurgents have cost us too much to overlook any of their supporters."

"Gobbling up a handful of smaller neighbors will do that," Dresden commented.

"He's right, you know," Aeneas interjected. "Might have been easy to beat the armies of the small kingdoms, but hell hath no fury like a conquered people."

"As much as I would love to discuss current events with all of you, I think we have more pressing matters to attend to. Wouldn't you agree?" Ostro suggested.

Not another word was said on the subject as the expedition continued up the road.

Abandoned tents began to appear along the road. Soon, whole encampments were found that suggested at one point there had been a large operation present. They noticed the tents were uniform in appearance and placement, a detail that was not lost on Ostro. As they pushed forward, the expedition finally came to a cave with crates of equipment stacked around its immense opening.

"What in the name of the Gods is all this?" Aeneas wondered.

"I'd guess some kind of mining operation," Dresden suggested.

"Aye, something of that kind," William concurred as he observed the contents of a crate he found opened. "A damned shit ton of bang bang over here."

"A ton of what?" Alexander asked.

"Dynooomite, sonny. A whole lot of it. Enough crates here to bring down half a city, if you don't mind me saying," William commented.

"Explosives, got it," Alexander said.

"Even if this was a mining operation, there still shouldn't be any dynamite. Stuff is beyond illegal," Dresden said.

"Indeed," Ostro confirmed. "Paints a rather suspicious picture."

"A problem I'm sure you and your people will have fun dealing with. But for now, the who and why of these people isn't relevant to me," Aeneas said.

"We got more of them scratches on the rock leading into the cave, sir," one of the soldiers pointed out.

"Guess whatever is down there took out a whole hell of a lot of people," Dresden said. "Maybe we could do something with this dynamite while we're here."

"Detonate and collapse the cave?" Aeneas guessed.

"Why not? We got enough here to do the job and then some," Dresden argued.

"After we find our people," Aeneas said. "William, you're our residential Sapper, think you can rig this entrance to blow at a moment's notice?"

"That I can, sir. And with great pleasure. I'd just need a few folks with me to assist in speeding the process along. Could have it done by the time you get back," William confirmed.

"Right, I'll leave a few to help. If we're not back in three hours, blow it regardless," Aeneas ordered.

"Whoa, hey, now," Ostro protested. "We don't know how deep that cave is; it could take us three hours just to get where we need to be."

"I'm not having them wait here forever!" Aeneas argued. "If you feel so nervous, then you can stay here with them and help set up the bombs."

"He's going with us," Alexander said. "Period."

Aeneas agreed and assigned some men to stay to help set the explosives. As the rest of the group prepared their equipment, Tom had silently moved closer to the cave entrance. He stared into the black cave in a blank state.

One of the soldiers pointed out Tom's movement away from the group to Aeneas, who tried, in vain, to call him back. As his calls went unheard, Aeneas prepared to approach Tom, but stopped in his tracks when Tom turned around. His eyes were black as the night and his face looked as though he had been hypnotized. Aeneas called to him again, but there was no response.

Finally, Tom turned his attention to Alexander and uttered in an alien voice, "See what you've wrought, Warden?" In the blink of an eye Tom was pulled by an invisible force into the cave and he disappeared from sight into the blackness.

CHAPTER 25
OUR LOSSES

U pon seeing his soldier get pulled into the cave, Aeneas sprinted into the darkness without a moment's hesitation. Cries from his men to slow down or stop went unheeded as they sprinted after him, their breathing becoming sporadic and shallow the deeper they went into the tunnel. Only a few of the men had torches, which caused many of them to misstep and trip on the uneven ground.

Alexander had no trouble keeping pace with everyone else, but resisted the urge to lead the charge without the help of torches. The path began to go downhill, and the moist nature of the cave played havoc on the expedition's footing. Suddenly, the lead man fell, starting a chain reaction that caused the whole group to tumble down the length of the cave. Their momentum was stopped by a series of boulders that lined an even path at the bottom of their decent.

As they all regained their footing after the hard landing, Alexander was first to notice Aeneas. He stood before an arch covered in symbols that resembled the ones that appeared on his body. Its material was dark, much darker than the rock around it, and the geometry suggested it had been built a long time ago rather than being part of the cave itself. Beyond the arch, there was a fissure in the rock that indicated a room. Through the hole, they could see more structures made of the same substance, lit by a glow of unknown origin.

"What do you make of this?" Aeneas asked, without looking back to see who approached.

Alexander responded hesitantly, "Haven't a clue."

None of the others had words to describe what was in front of them either. The place was so incredibly alien that it was no shock to believe that creatures as unnatural as the Screechers would spawn from it.

The markings along the walls suggested that this was excavated by a mining operation. As the men discussed the discovery, someone said the ruins uncovered might have been the catalyst for the appearance of the Screechers. But, none of it mattered to the lot of them, they were here to discover the fate of their comrades and hopefully save as many as possible.

Without a moment to lose, Aeneas led them under the arch and through the fissure where the walls turned upward and the area opened up into monumental proportions. It was like walking into another world, as though a whole city was built underground, with buildings of varying heights existing under a ceiling that towered so high it was barely visible. However, in the distance, an enormous ruby hung from the ceiling, serving the purpose of a sun that led a crimson glow to the atmosphere. In a remarkable discovery, the walls that bordered the entire vault were smooth as glass, not an imperfection to be seen.

"It's so perfect," Alexander commented in awe. "How is this possible?"

"No machine can do this, none that I've ever seen," Dresden said. "These buildings, their design, Alex—"

"I know." Alexander quickly answered. Their design was the same as the ones where he gained his mysterious powers.

Alexander took the lead in the exploration. Areas were lit by a series of amber stones that lined various structures in patterns that formed a language of some kind. Buildings were situated in a pattern that centered on a large rectangular structure with elaborate patterns carved into its architecture. Each column and portico that extended from the structure emitted an aura designed to intimidate, and that feeling was felt by every person who took in the immense structure.

Alexander felt as though someone was watching him, and the feeling guided him to look at the roofs of the surrounding buildings. He could not see what gave him the feeling but was drawn to the entrance of the main structure.

"In there." Alexander pointed. "That's where they are."

Alexander led the way inside the structure after climbing the outside stairs. The interior opened to a lobby lined with tall columns and statues of extraordinary individuals in heroic poses. The interior was made of the same black mineral that absorbed the light the torches gave off. The only source of light was a series of lamps lit by blue flames that added an ominous feel to the atmosphere. The dancing shadows of objects caused even the most hardened soldier to flinch as the group proceeded further inside. At the center of the lobby was an immense statue of an individual dressed in extravagant armor, holding a sword high into the air. Behind the statue was a wide staircase that led to the upper levels.

"Help me!" a voice cried from atop the staircase. The group saw that it was Tom, bloodied and frantic. He limped down the stairs at a furious pace. "Help me!" he yelled again.

Aeneas bolted around the statue and caught the man as he fell down the last few steps. He lowered him slowly to the ground and comforted him in an effort to calm him down.

"It's all right, son," Aeneas said in a clam voice. "What happened to you? What happened to everyone else?"

"Who is it?" one of the soldiers inquired.

"It's Tom," Aeneas answered. "What happened?"

Tom was shaken and unable to utter a word without a stutter. "Showed…me."

"He's delirious," Dresden commented.

"What? What do you mean, showed you? Showed you what?" Aeneas pressed.

Tom slowed his breaths and stared blankly. "Showed me the darkness." Tom began to writhe in intense pain. His eyes began to bleed and his mouth foamed.

"Seizure!" Aeneas yelled. "Give me something for his mouth!"

Some men proceeded to help Aeneas with their comrade's condition, but were taken aback when Tom's skin began to blister and boil with puss-filled cysts. His body began to convulse violently. Alexander pulled Aeneas away once they realized this was no seizure.

"Get back!" Dresden yelled.

As everyone stepped away from the body, the convulsions became more violent until they suddenly stopped. Aeneas started towards the body until he was stopped by the sight of Tom's chest splitting open. A black mist shot out of the cavity to everyone's shock. It lingered in the air before its form turned into a Screecher. Silently it glared at the group. When it noticed Alexander, the creature hissed before disappearing into the ceiling.

"What—" Alexander started.

"You think anyone has an answer to that?" Dresden interrupted.

Aeneas regained himself after his experience. "If Tom just got here and that happened to him…"

"I know what you're thinking, but we at least owe them a look around… since we're already here," Dresden suggested.

"And we know that this is where they were likely taken," Alexander added. "We should make our way upstairs."

Despite initial calls for an early exit, the search continued to the upper levels. An elaborate mural decorated the wall at the top of the staircase, depicting a towering individual standing above a crowd of followers who bowed in worship. The figure held a sword in one hand and a shield in the other. Alexander stopped to examine the shield as the rest of the group moved on. Dresden went back to collect Alexander as he fell behind.

"What is it?" Dresden asked.

Alexander, a little taken aback, shook his head. "Nothing, just looking." He went to rejoin the others while Dresden took a quick glance at the area before returning to the fold. Although it was a quick glance, Dresden was quick to notice that the shield bore the same markings as Alexander's.

Men kept so close to one another that they often bumped shoulders, causing one or both to jump. Nerves built up enough in every man that they could not help but get spooked by even the thought of something they couldn't see touching them.

Several rooms lined the corridor that hauntingly echoed the steps of the party. Although they were on a search and rescue mission, no one made it a priority to actually poke their head into any of the rooms.

Dresden stopped the party to voice his annoyance that no one was searching. Aeneas was hesitant to send any of his men into the rooms, as he feared they might not come out. As the two went back and forth in argument, Alexander decided to step away from the group to explore a room close by.

Inside the room, he didn't find anything of interest other than some elaborate and strange furniture that made him scoff at the thought of it being comfortable. However, his eye was caught by a painting that seemed to appear on the wall when he wasn't looking.

"Odd, wasn't there before," he muttered as he went to get a closer look. It was a colorful picture of a city skyline with tall buildings and a view of streets full of people. Alexander was impressed, as he never saw what the cities were like below the clouds. The last he knew, humans still lived behind walls. An uneasy feeling gripped Alexander, causing him to turn around to leave only to discover the doorway was gone. The room was sealed with no way out. Alexander rushed to where the exit was and pounded on the wall.

"This can't be real," he nervously muttered to himself before another feeling came over him and caused him to turn back around. The painting had changed. As he walked closer, the buildings had lost their color, structures were damaged or completely destroyed, fires raged, the sky was black, and the streets were empty of people.

On the floor of the room Alexander noticed a small plaque that seemed to come from the bottom of the painting. He picked it up to find that it read, *Haven*. The picture had changed again when he looked back. This time the city was in even more dire conditions, but one detail caught Alexander's eye and the uneasy feeling that had plagued him before returned. It was a small detail, but Alexander found a small figure lying in one of the streets, surrounded by blood, and a desperate-looking figure trying to reach out to it from the cover of an alleyway.

This is impossible.

The sound of a loud gunshot rang out behind Alexander, who quickly drew his weapons and turned to meet the source. However, everything changed. The dark dreary room had turned into an alley that led to an open street. A group had stumbled over to his side of the street while another group prepared to follow. Alexander noticed a familiar woman among those who had just crossed and spotted a man on the other side who picked up a small girl and prepared to cross the street.

"No wait!" Alexander yelled, but found that no one noticed his presence. Before he could physically do anything, the next group ran across the street.

"No!" Another shot echoed and the man holding the girl dropped her to the ground. The man was dead. But the girl was not. The mother screamed in horror at the sight and had to be held back by multiple people as she tried to get to her daughter.

Alexander couldn't speak, couldn't think. He could not believe what he saw. But the sounds, the horrific sounds of a sobbing mother trying to console a daughter who screamed in pain for her mom made him drop to his knees. In vain, he blocked his ears to stop the sounds from coming through, to no avail.

"I can see all your fears," an ominous voice said.

Angered by the perceived taunt amidst the tragic background, Alexander rose to his feet with his weapons, ready to lash out. "Show yourself! What do you want from me?"

"No amount of strength can save you, Reclaimer."

"Why do you call me that? I don't know what that is." Alexander questioned.

"I know you do not, but with that mark you carry their sins. This place has shown me what the people who bore that mark have done to this world. Although long forgotten, their memory is fresh here and now."

"What do want from me? You want me to die? Then do it!" Alexander demanded.

"Death is easy. In death, one is blind, unable to see consequence."

"Consequence of what?" Alexander questioned as he spun around to find whoever was speaking to him. Then the landscape changed again to an open field surrounded by high black walls in the distance. The ground was soft and muddy from a recent rain that fell from the cloudy sky. Alexander felt a push from a man who ran into him. The man's appearance was a shock to Alexander, as he was so skinny that his eyes were sunk into his skull and his arms were nothing but skin and bones. The man was scared beyond reason at the sight of Alexander and tried to crawl away as fast as he could. Alexander's gestures for help only further terrified the man.

Another man, muscular and covered in markings, walked over and stabbed the man to death with his blade. The murderer's markings began to glow, and he let out a thunderous howl from the boost he appeared to get with the kill.

"What the hell is wrong with you?" Alexander screamed at the top of his lungs.

"Easy now, brother. Plenty more to choose from," the marked man said with a smile.

Alexander struggled to comprehend what had just happened. He was only able to whimper, "Brother?" His attention was immediately drawn by grotesque sounds along with cries, howls, and other horrific things. He would never forget what he saw, a seemingly endless field, mass murder of scores of people by those who bore those familiar markings.

"*Noble Wardens,*" the voice sarcastically mocked, "All your morals, all your strength was not enough to keep your people from crumbling to the temptation of dark magic. Your people's abuse of Essence…is what banished you all from this world."

This can't be true.

Meanwhile, Dresden and the rest of the men were in a frantic search for the missing Warden. Aeneas finally ordered his men to sweep every room they found because he knew full well that Alexander was the only person who could give them a chance at survival.

Aeneas grew frustrated by the lack of results. "No one just up and vanishes like that!"

"After what we saw today, I doubt anything would surprise me now," Ostro commented, to the surprise of everyone.

"Thought you lost your ability to speak for a while there," Dresden jabbed.

"Certain times call for observation rather than talk," Ostro shot back.

Aeneas took count of the men who came back from their search, becoming worried when he realized a couple were missing. "Where are the rest of the men? Darius! Colion!"

Screams echoed down the corridor as he called their names.

"They shouldn't be down that far. C'mon!" Aeneas led a charge in the direction of the screams. Dresden and Ostro guarded the rear as the others rounded the corner and were shocked to find the men had disappeared and they were alone.

"They were just here!" Ostro yelped. "What do we do now?"

A bright light emanated down the corridor where they believed the others went. The light grew so intense that it became blinding. Dresden glimpsed a figure on the ground. Something about the sight called him to walk toward the figure against Ostro's protests.

"What are you doing? Haven't you ever heard of not walking into the light?" Ostro protested.

However, Dresden was called forward by an alluring sense of familiarity. His senses were calmed by the light, but as he drew closer, the calm turned to a sense of urgency. He picked up the pace as the figure transformed to a person. Still holding up the rear, Ostro became increasingly nervous at the sounds of distant explosions drawing closer. Now tremors shook the floor. He forced himself to move forward out of fear of being left alone.

The figure was covered from head to toe in sleek, metallic armor. Dresden stood above the body, his exposed facial features still as stone. The armor of the mysterious body was covered in charred burn marks and blood spewed from multiple stab wounds. This person was in dire straits and struggled with every breath. Emotionless, Dresden knelt next to the body, his composure still intact.

Ostro, however, had nothing but questions about the situation. "What is this?"

"An illusion, a memory… meant to provoke for some reason," Dresden reasoned.

"A memory of what?"

"Of the worst day of my life. When I lost my last teammate, when I had to leave her behind as our Order fell," Dresden explained.

"Can't imagine the point of all this." Ostro examined his surroundings in suspicion. "Don't really want to see anything from my past."

"I've seen worse in my life, tenfold. But this one is the one that hit me the most." Dresden stood back up and let out a sigh. "Clearly, whatever force is here has enough spite and suffering that it wants everyone else to suffer by showing people their biggest fears."

"Pretty calm for facing your worst moment," Ostro said.

"It hurts, but I know this isn't real," Dresden said as the vision faded away and the area returned to normal when the light finally extinguished. "Fear only has power if you decide to feed it."

"Well, that's all well and good philosophically, but that doesn't explain the lad we saw decompose in front of our eyes," Ostro replied referring to Tom's fate.

"Who knows, could be something else at work, maybe it was a vision, who knows at the end of it all? I can only imagine what everyone else is going through, especially Alex."

Ostro took note of a wall that had unusual markings on it. He went over to examine it with caution, as he did not want to get sucked into a vision of his own. The examination caused Ostro enough concern to call Dresden over to have a look. The markings were a series of hieroglyphs that told a story of the builders of this place. There were depictions of men that came from the sky who protected all civilized life from monsters, these beings were concluded to be Wardens.

However, the images showed that the Wardens split into different sects along the way. One protected and the other hunted and killed people as they worshipped the depiction of a skull. The markings surrounding this more murderous sect were the same that they saw on

Alexander. A war between the two sides was depicted and showed the skull worshippers being defeated. In their defeat, the skull-worshiping Wardens sacrificed themselves to create a red orb containing their power. It was stored in a temple hidden deep in a forest. After their victory, the other Wardens left the world for good.

"I've never heard this story," Ostro said, astonished by what he saw.

"Neither have I, but I guess it would explain why the Wardens left so long ago. This being shown to us is too convenient, don't you think?" Dresden suggested.

Ostro looked over to notice that an additional scene had appeared. "If you thought that was unbelievable…" Ostro's voice trailed off in shock as he pointed out the new drawing to Dresden.

"We have to find him. Now," Dresden said with a sense of urgency.

They both turned and ran back to where they might find Alexander, for the last picture on the wall depicted the abandoned temple that housed the red orb. This time, it had a visitor.

Chapter 26
Darkness

Alexander angrily pounded the muddy ground, trying desperately to block the sights and sounds that lay before him. His tear-filled eyes could not stand to witness any more. As the noise continued to slip through, the anger began to take a toll on his senses. "Stop this!" he demanded forcefully. "Stop this now!" There was no response to his demands, but the sounds started to dissipate and soon silence reigned.

"Ask and you shall receive, Warden." The voice had changed to a more familiar tone, one that Alexander recognized. He picked his head up and immediately began to search around for the source. As he searched, the light dimmed and Alexander found himself blinded by darkness. A lone light flickered above him farther ahead.

The area had been transformed again. Alexander found himself traversing a hill to reach the distant glow. Rain began to fall as he climbed higher up the muddy hill. Darkness narrowed his path to a single route, as he did not dare step into the unknown off to his sides. The hill became a mountain in scale and it was difficult to push on through the muck. The ground leveled out as he reached the top, but the glow appeared to retreat farther in the distance until it finally disappeared.

The darkness was broken by a flash of lightning. To Alexander's shock, the flash revealed that he was surrounded by a sea of corpses. Another flash revealed that the bodies were the soldiers from Aeneas' unit. The dim glow returned, but Alexander's attention was caught by the identity of the corpses. One by one, he found those he feared to find. Aeneas lay with his throat slit beside his men, who had also been cut down by blades. A rush of adrenaline came over him as he sprinted toward the sight of the bodies of those he'd come to know.

"Dresden… Mira."

Another flash of light revealed a silhouette near Alexander. He jumped to his feet to find the silhouette in full charge at him. Alexander drew his blade in barely enough time to block the incoming strike. The strength from the enemy's blade overpowered him. The force that Alexander had to summon to push back almost drained him of all his energy. There was only a brief moment of respite before the figure swung again. Alexander, again, blocked the attack. Both sides struggled to overwhelm each other through pure physical force.

As Alexander pushed back, he looked right into the face of his opponent. He eyes were drawn to the butt of his opponent's blade and a horrific sense of familiarity penetrated his thoughts. A flash of lightning became a moment of stark revelation as the light revealed his opponent to be himself. Eyes red as fire, hairless, a pale face and covered in the markings that plagued his body and dreams.

"Look upon yourself Warden, this is your fate. A form of pure evil, corruption, just like your ancestors so long as you stay in this world. The spell that churns inside you will soon overtake you and you will know nothing but slaughter," the voice prophesized.

"No!" he yelled. The sight of himself as his opponent caused Alexander to let his guard down, which prompted his other self to punch him with a force that threw him backwards.

As he hit the ground, the force seemed to act like a switch that transformed the world back to what it was. Without a thought, Alexander jumped to his feet and scanned the area for another attack. But, instead of an enemy, he found Mira lying on the ground, motionless. Alexander rushed to her side and found she was unconscious and that the phantom stood not far away.

"What have you done to her?" Alexander demanded.

"Nothing of harm. I only showed her the memory that pains you the most. The truth," the phantom said.

Alexander shuttered and tried to deflect away from the memory, "…I know you're trying to crossover to The Abyss."

"As are you. For more personal and foolish reasons," the phantom responded.

"Warden," Mira whimpered as she slowly woke.

"Your friend is committed to your cause. Seeking the soul of your lost love," the phantom said. "How honorable, especially after how she came to pass."

Before Alexander's eyes, Emily appeared opposite the phantom in her white dress, holding a small bag. She was a sight to behold. Her presence brought Alexander great pain as she stood there and stared at him with despair and worry. The air had turned brisk with her appearance, and Alexander saw his breath pass between his lips. This scene of Emily standing next to the phantom left him with a sense of familiarity, for his dreams had depicted this very thing.

The specter of Emily walking towards him with ghostly grace and a tired, defeated expression on her face made Alexander shudder. She drew closer and nearly knocked him off balance as she walked right through him. He watched her move away and then a statue of heroic Wardens seemed to appear out of nowhere.

"No! No I can't watch this!" Alexander cried, "Stop!" But his cries were of no use, like in his dreams. Emily's golden blonde hair, gentle face, and blue eyes were amplified by well-done makeup and a snow white dress. Her appearance took Alexander's breath away. Emily sat on the ground against the base of the statue and stared into the sky. Silently she pulled out a dagger from her bag and held it tight. Alexander's grip on Mira tightened which caused her to flinch. A lone tear rolled from Emily's eye, causing her mascara to smear slightly.

Mira slowly became more alert. "Did she?"

Tears dripped from Alexander's shut eyes as he tried to ignore the scene that played out in front of him. Finally, he summoned enough strength to utter in crackled voice, "Yes, she did." In a blink of an eye, Emily took the dagger to her wrists without any hesitation and then leaned back against the statue as the life drained from her. Alexander closed his eyes tightly and whispered "No" to himself over and over.

"This world is pain, isn't it, Warden?" the phantom said as the vision of Emily's decision faded away. "One that doesn't care for our existence or our pain. The only saving grace was the goodness of people to make it all just a little bit easier. But that does not exist anymore. This world is dead. And I will take it to its rightful place in The Abyss, like all the other souls that came to pass."

"No. You can't!" Alexander cried as he rose to his feet, only to see the phantom disappear.

"Meet me here if you wish to stop me," the voice echoed.

"What do you mean here? I am here! I—" Alexander was interrupted by the transformation of his surroundings. The distant walls charged forward at a feverish pace, prompting Alexander to close his eyes in anticipation of being crushed. The thunder of the approaching walls stopped, and he opened his eyes to find himself in the same room he had entered. Mira recovered and brought herself to her feet.

"I'm so sorry, Alex," she said.

"Maybe she was right; I should have stayed," Alexander admitted.

"What do you mean?"

"She's been appearing to me the whole time I've been here. Used to be in dreams, but then I started seeing her in real life. All she would say to me was that I should have stayed." He put his hand over his face. "And that thing knew it. It's been using it against me, mocking me, drawing me to this trap. I left everything behind, my home, everyone I've known. Just for a chance to see her again."

"Can't blame yourself. Many would have done the same thing for someone they cared about. No matter the obstacles," Mira said in an effort to comfort him.

Their conversation was interrupted by Dresden and Ostro running through the door with their weapons at the ready, pointed at Alexander. Mira was astonished by the show of force that seemed to come from nowhere.

"Mira!" Dresden was shocked that they had found her along with Alexander. "Step away from him!"

Mira was left stumped. "Why? What's going on?"

"The Warden is dangerous," Ostro explained. "His markings are part of some curse that carries the powers of a sect of his people that were like some kind of genocidal death cult."

"What?" Alexander was shocked by the assertion. "Never have there been any death cults with my people, at least to my knowledge. Dresden, that phantom is here; he's going to try and open a gateway to The Abyss."

"Isn't that what you're trying to do?" Dresden questioned.

"Well, yeah, but that thing's goal is to make the world into The Abyss. It's trying to destroy the world!" Alexander yelled in frustration as he noticed their guns were still aimed at him. "We've got to stop this!"

"Alex, I know what you are, even if you don't. That mark carries a monstrous legacy of death," Dresden said.

"I know," Alexander admitted. "I was shown what they did to people. But, I'm not them! The threat is real, and it's that damned phantom."

"We can't trust him," Ostro said to Dresden and Mira. "Whatever his motivations were, we must assume they've been corrupted by whatever curse he carries."

"Stop this!" Mira yelled. "We need to focus on the real danger."

The building shook from a thunderous tremor that knocked everyone off balance. Alexander seized the opportunity and threw his shield at Ostro, knocking him to the ground, and charged Dresden and sliced his rifle in half. Mira knocked Dresden down with a punch to the stomach and head when he tried to maneuver around Alexander. Once both were on the floor, Alexander and Mira made their escape.

"Where do we go?" Mira asked as they ran.

Alexander felt a strengthening of some force in the air as the ground continued to shake. "The field behind the wall!"

The two made a quick escape out of the building in the direction where they saw a tall black wall. Beyond the wall, the massive ruby in the high ceiling glowed a deep red. As they ran closer, there was no entrance to be seen along the massive stretch of wall. Instead of slowing down, Alexander sped up, to the surprise of a slowing Mira. She called for him to stop, but he did not heed her calls.

Instead he ran straight into the wall and crashed through. The force created a hole that allowed Mira to follow beyond the wall. On the other side, the phantom stood before a portal.

"Warden," the phantom said. "I hoped you would come see the final moments of the world. A pleasure for you, I'm sure."

"What kind of person wants the world to just cease?" Alexander asked.

"A person who saw everything this world has come to and all that it will become. For years, I wandered the world in search of some light that would make me think there is hope for this world. There is no future, just death. I plan to shorten the path, and with it, cut out all the suffering that will come before the world breathes its last," the phantom explained.

"Why not just kill yourself? End it all for you rather than decide the fate of everyone else?" Mira questioned.

"Suicide is painless for me, true. But it would be selfish to remove myself when I know I could end everyone's suffering. That's why I built this, to do one thing and one thing only, bring The Abyss here. Have you looked at the world you walk in? A world consumed by the darkness of the Long Night, a harbinger of the end." The phantom turned its attention to Alexander. "Emily knew what the true nature of the world was, what *people* really were. She had nobody."

Alexander burst out in anger, "She had me!"

"Had you, until you turned your back on her."

"I've had enough of this and your invasions of my thoughts! You just want an audience for the end of the world?" Alexander questioned.

"No, turns out I need you." The phantom gestured with his hand and the ground began to lighten into the shape of a pentagram. "A sea of blood from normal humans isn't enough to open this portal alone. The villagers, the passing detachment of soldiers, your compatriots, they weren't enough to satisfy the conditions. A small offering of blood with the purest of Essence is what I need to finish the process. This compass is filled with such raw power, alas it needs the key that is your blood to fully unlock it."

The lights in the ground reached out like vines and grabbed Alexander by the wrists and legs. He was constrained and forced to his knees. Mira attempted to cut the vines of light with her sword, but when she made contact, she was electrocuted by the energy and thrown back. She lay on the ground, motionless.

"Mira!" Alexander yelled.

"Don't worry, you'll see her again soon." The phantom walked up to Alexander with a blade in its hand, then knelt and sliced a cut down his face to draw blood. Alexander screamed in pain as the blade finished its job. "If not for you, this wouldn't be possible."

"Who are you? Just tell me who you are," Alexander pleaded.

"My name is Karahia, father of six dead children, husband of one dead wife, and a member of one dead race of mages."

"Vengeance has consumed you," Alexander growled.

"I wasn't always like this my friend, there was a time I was just a simple mage trying to make his way in the world. But the madness of weak-minded people cast me as an evil that needed to be purged, same for my family. After the lights of my life were snuffed out, my quest for meaning began. Who knew it would be the kind people of the nearby village that showed me the truth that lies here."

"The people showed you this place?"

"That they did, believing a mage was needed to investigate this mysterious place. Within this place, I encountered a force similar to what you encountered. Granted I had a more…severe reaction to it. But, the voices that spawned from it showed me your people's past, their power, the secrets to accessing the other realms beyond our own, and so much more."

"Other realms?" Alexander whispered to himself.

"So, with all this knowledge bestowed upon me, I used it to create this gateway to link our world with The Abyss."

Karahia proceeded to the gateway he had constructed with the compass he had stolen from Alexander some time ago and just smeared with his blood. He placed the compass before the gateway structure that lay at the center of the pentagram. As he did so, the ground lit up even brighter. Karahia uttered a few chants in an unknown language that made the ground dance with life and the giant ruby above project a beam of energy that struck the portal. The red energy swirled in the structure as it began to take form.

Meanwhile, Alexander had resigned himself to defeat as his body stopped fighting the restraints.

"*Alex,*" a voice called from the developing portal.

"Emily?"

"*Alex, stop him,*" she said.

"I can't."

"*Yes, you can. Use your strength.*"

"Not without becoming like those monsters," Alexander explained.

"Be better than them, please!" she pleaded.

Alexander's concentration was cut short by Karahia's screech. Mira had awoken, snuck up and cut off one of Karahia's arms. To her surprise, he knocked her away with one swing of his hand and pulled out a sword as he walked to where she laid, defenseless.

"Pathetic brute," Karahia said in anger. "I may not be skilled with a blade, but it'll be enough to gut you."

Alexander began to yell in anger, his veins popping from his skin as he slowly rose to his feet. Still restrained, his feet dug into the ground as the restraints wrestled with his strength. His skin began to burn as he knew the markings had returned. Deep down, he felt the raw power, energy, and emotion of this ancestral power as it began to flow through his body. Although he resisted the desire to fully embrace it, Alexander tapped just enough of it to overpower his restraints.

Karahia turned to see what was transpiring. "It's too late," he reminded Alexander as the gateway began to take its final form, "Once formed, it can't be closed."

Suddenly, Alexander's bonds broke, his sword and shield returned to his hands. His eyes turned blood red with rage. Now free, he charged forward. Surprised, Karahia fired a series of energy blasts that had to be blocked by a shield. Clearly, he was stalling for time. Knowing he was being bogged down by ranged assaults, Alexander broke to the right and used his shield as a projectile. The shield struck Karahia, knocking him off balance and Alexander plunged his sword into Karahia's abdomen.

Karahia did not scream like he did when his arm was severed; he did not react to the stab at all. Instead, he calmly fell to the ground with a strange grace with Alexander still atop him. In his last moments,

Karahia's elfin face was revealed from under his hood. His skin was pale, his face featured many scars, and his ears had been mutated to mimic human ears. Karahia's eyes were pitch black, and stared at Alexander as he struggled with his final breaths. Then he died.

Alexander lowered his body slowly to the ground and found that both his hands bore the markings. A shockwave shot out from the gateway as it was completed.

"Alex." Mira ran over. "The portal, it's open, we've got to close it."

"*Alex*," Emily cried out.

Alexander moved toward the gateway with Mira following.

"Alex, you can't save her, don't try it. You heard him, this thing was built to bring everything here, not just her," Mira argued.

"Idolon told me there was a chance I could pull her through and then destroy it." Alexander proceeded toward the portal.

"Who the hell is Idolon?" Mira grabbed Alexander's arm. "You can't do this! I'm destroying this thing!"

Mira rushed ahead with her sword drawn and prepared to strike the base of the portal. Her sword was stopped by Alexander's hand. In shock, she saw that Alexander's hands bore those markings and his eyes had turned red. Before she could react to the block, Alexander punched her in the stomach, denting her armor, and pulled the sword away from her. Mira regained herself and attempted to attack Alexander, but he blocked her attack and laid a powerful strike to her head with the butt of her own sword. A follow up punch to her chest sent her flying back to the ground.

Without anyone in his way, Alexander went to stand before the portal. The voices of all the dead echoed through his mind as he searched the gateway for any sign of Emily. Miraculously, her face began to form in the swirl of energy. He simply stood there as his eyes transitioned from red to blue. His mind raced.

"Emily, what do I do?"

The roar of the gateway became deafening. Alexander did not hear as Dresden and Ostro approached the area. They came across an injured Mira, who was coughing up blood and barely conscious. Dresden checked on Mira as Ostro aimed his weapon at Alexander who stood in front of the portal.

"Mira." Dresden tried to wake her up. "What happened?"

"Stop him," she whimpered.

"Don't worry, you already did. Just rest," Dresden said in an attempt to comfort her after seeing the dark figure lie lifeless on the floor.

"No!" Her voice crackled. "The Warden, stop Alex." Despite her struggle, she was not able to say much more before once more losing consciousness.

Emily's face became more and more real with every passing moment. Alexander stood there, torn about what to do with this chance. His attempts at conversation went unanswered, while the voices got even stronger. He felt the wave of forces coming from The Abyss. The air already felt as though the whole world had frozen over. At this moment, when he saw Emily more alive than ever, he felt a sense of hopelessness. As if this was too good to be real.

"*Alex,*" Emily called.

"Yes?" Alexander answered.

"*I was so sad.*"

"Why? Why? What made you so sad?" Alexander cried.

"*I couldn't expect you to understand,*" she said.

"No, I want to understand. I'm so sorry I wasn't there, I betrayed your friendship and trust. That's all I ever wanted was to understand you and why you made the decision you did!" Alexander pleaded with her, tears running down his face. Emily was silent at the plea. "Please, Emily! I'm so sorry!"

"*Alex, I-*" Emily's voice was stopped by the sound of a bullet cracking through the air and breaking the base that held the structure for the gateway. The rest of it fell to the ground and shattered, causing the energy built up to explode with a force that threw Alexander several feet in the air. The energy used to create the gateway shot up into the air and crashed into the ruby causing a tremor to ripple through the ceiling. Around the ruby, a vortex of excess energy began to swirl and the strength of the tremors caused a series of cracks to form across the ceiling.

In a daze, Alexander rose to find Emily gone and Dresden holding a rifle in the distance, smoke still billowing from the barrel. Numbness crawled up Alexander's spine, his head began to pound and he became overcome with intense anger. He charged at them in a blind fury. Dresden was only able to get a few shots off before Alexander disarmed him and bludgeoned him with his rifle.

Ostro tried to throw a punch, but was thrown to the ground and knocked out by a crushing blow. Alexander felt a stab in his side. Unfazed, he turned to find Dresden had shoved one of his hidden blades between a gap in his armor. Noticing it was ineffective, Dresden quickly shoved his other blade into Alexander. But it was no use. Alexander spun around and tackled Dresden and began to pummel his head.

"You took her from me, bastard!" he yelled as he threw down punches that would crush a man's skull if it wasn't for the armor Dresden wore on his head. Even though his armor was only dented, Dresden lost consciousness.

Kill him.

As quickly as he started, Alexander stopped his own assault. He stood up over the bodies around him and grabbed his fist in disbelief at what he had done. Pure dread entered his mind as Alexander realized that whatever spell was inside him was slowly entering his thoughts and pushing him over the edge. It was only a matter of time until the vision of himself he'd seen earlier became a reality.

Look upon yourself Warden, this is your fate. A form of pure evil, corruption, just like your ancestors as long as you stay in this world. The spell that churns inside you will soon overtake you, and you will know nothing but slaughter.

"What have I become? What *will* I become?" Alexander asked himself.

"Warden!" Aeneas approached with five of his men. "What happened here?"

Alexander looked around for a moment to gather his thoughts. "We took down the monster responsible for all this. They all are hurt pretty bad; we've got to get them out of here. This place is about to cave in!"

"All right, we'll get them out. Let's move, men!"

"I'll take Dresden; you get the other two. C'mon, we're running out of time," Alexander ordered. As he went to grab Dresden, a thunderous shockwave roared from the vortex. Beams of red energy flowed into the ground, twisting around like frenzied snakes that devoured each other in an endless cycle. The energy slowly joined together to form another portal.

"Oh no, it's become self-sustaining." Alexander observed.

"What's become self-sustaining, the portal? How?" Aeneas questioned nervously.

"Don't know, must have only needed to be formed initially, but now can hold itself together on its own."

"What do we do?"

Alexander focused on the portal, trying to find a solution to the problem. The power of the gateway consumed his vision so much that the rest of the world turned black to him and he felt a deep emptiness filled with a sea of dust and the echoes of eternity. A foreboding danger crept into his mind and Alexander knew the malevolent soul of the Abyss drew nearer. Although no one could truly know what was coming, Alexander felt the terror of an endless realm of death approach.

A burning desire flows in your veins. I feel it. It grows ever hotter. It will consume you.

Alexander noticed his compass nearby and retrieved it, then opened it to see if fate thought differently than the deepest sense of duty he felt weighing heavily upon his chest. He sighed with a slight chuckle when he saw the arrow pointed directly at the portal. "May not be able to stop all fires, but this one…this one is mine," Alexander muttered to himself. He closed the compass and stared at his hands with an expression of acceptance and then said, "Get Dresden and Mira out of here, I'll close the portal."

"Wait, what? This place is gonna cave in, you'll die, let's just let the portal get buried!" Aeneas yelled.

"Can't risk it, I have to do this." Alexander turned to Aeneas and threw him the compass that had guided him here. "Go, now!"

Aeneas nodded in agreement as his group grabbed the wounded Mira, Dresden and Ostro before they made their escape. Massive pieces of the cavern ceiling began falling to the ground with such force that it crushed the ancient structures. As Dresden was carried away he awoke for a moment and through the haze covering his vision, he saw the distant silhouette of Alexander slowly approach the portal. Then he passed out.

The sheer power that emanated from the portal churned winds that would knock structures down, but not Alexander. Without weapons he approached ever closer to the portal that seemed to call to his soul while simultaneously repelling his body. Winds flowing outward from the portal carried the ever louder cries and echoes of the dead in languages older than time itself. A small hope flickered in Alexander's mind that one of these voices was Emily's, but it was impossible to cut through all the noise. Each step felt like a mile deeper into a burning fire that made the air hotter and hotter the closer he drew.

The seemingly endless journey ended suddenly with Alexander standing before the portal that pulsed and rippled violently as all of The Abyss tried to break into the world.

All right. Now, what in the name of the Goddesses do I do?

As he raised his hands to the portal, a haunting chorus emanated from The Abyss that said the same thing, "You should have stayed." Alexander closed his eyes as the pain of his past crept in again at those words. The voices grew louder and Alexander's hands grew hot from the spell inside him that wanted to take control after being let out to defeat Karahia. All the voices filled his head, repeating the same words over and over, faster and faster until there was no room for any of his own thoughts. Then, as if she cut a blade through all the other voices, Emily entered his mind, "I wish you stayed."

"I know," Alexander opened his eyes to reveal they'd turned red, signaling his full acceptance of the dark powers that churned within him and that he'd used during this desperate moment. "But, I'm here now." Without taking his eyes off the portal he raised his hand, from which emanated a power that pulled his sword to him off the ground. In one fluid motion he raised his sword above the portal with both hands. Before he struck, Alexander released himself to every aspect of the dark powers within. He felt the burns of the symbols leaving their mark upon him rise up his arms and across the rest of his body. His face became scarred with the symbols of the corrupted form of himself he'd seen in Karahia's vision. Before the corruption could take hold of his senses, Alexander used the last of his will to thrust his sword into the portal. The explosive reaction that followed filled the air instantaneously with an immeasurable force that collapsed the whole cavern, burying everything underneath.

The shockwave traveled at immense speed up the tunnel where Aeneas and his group neared the exit. The force threw the group into the air and out of the tunnel to William's surprise. As the entrance to the tunnel caved in, the ground shook and the group pulled themselves up and ran away to safety. The vibrations of the earth felt as though something tried to break through to the surface. Then they heard a loud crack from within. As Aeneas turned to see what it was, Dresden awoke to see what everyone else was witnessing. A golden beam of light pierced through the ground and shot into the clouds as if it were a pillar to the divine itself. The beam produced a thunder so immense that it shook the trees. Lightning began to spark and rage in the clouds surrounding the beam. The tremors and storm continued to escalate to a point where it felt as though the world was going to end, but in an instant the beam dissipated and the storm subsided. Aeneas marveled at what had happened and didn't notice that Dresden had regained himself enough to stand up next to him.

"Unbelievable," Aeneas gasped.

"From the depths of death, one will be risen to light the world," Dresden recalled to himself as a piece of naked sky broke through the cloud cover to the amazement of all who saw what just happened. Soon, another piece broke through, then another, until the clouds began to break throughout the sky. "Well, I'll be damned."

Epilogue

Clouds still lingered, but the darkness had been broken as the sun above lit the world for the first time in years. However joyous it was to behold the light, now the truly decrepit state of the world could be seen. Mira and Ostro recovered from their wounds and packed up enough supplies from the abandoned encampment for their own journeys. Ostro's amazement at the return of an orange tinted sky was overshadowed by the discovery that the abandoned camp was a staging ground for an army from Oren. The possibility of an entire Oren army being destroyed by Karahia was something that would have repercussions in the conflict. What they were exactly, no one knew.

Mira felt an overwhelming sense of peace in her heart as her father and the Endless Legend had been proven right. Hope entered her mind that perhaps her people had a future after all in this new world. As everyone prepared to part ways, Aeneas requested a moment with Dresden where he presented Alexander's compass to him.

"Here, I'm pretty sure the Warden wanted this to go to you," Aeneas said as he passed the item on to a silent Dresden. "So it's true that he really did that to you?"

"Yeah," Dresden acknowledged as he rubbed the dent in his mask. "He lost himself down there for a moment, but I guess he ended up making the right decision."

"A hard decision, to be sure. Temptation always has its victories over the best of us. The key though, is making sure those are only battles and not the whole war," Aeneas said as he examined a small green bud he'd noticed on a nearby tree branch. "Maybe the world will change from this."

Dresden took a closer look at the compass that held the power to show a person a path to their fate. He opened it to see that it spun around in all directions, almost unsure of where to settle. Dresden relaxed his mind and slowly sighed. To his surprise, the compass needle settled in a direction. "Perhaps the world will change, but the main question is, will we?"

"A great question," Aeneas said. "But that's for others to decide, Oren, Acropoli, the rest of them. Everyone is gonna be wondering what happened here to cause this." He glanced up at the sky to catch another glimpse of what was still mostly hidden by the layers of clouds. "What will you do now?"

"Was shown a vision down there…of something I thought I left in the past, something I was never going to forgive myself for, maybe might try to correct it….or at least make amends," Dresden said. "Perhaps his compass might show the way."

"You sound like a man who has quite the history," Aeneas commented.

"A colorful life is expected for a Green Blade Knight." Dresden admitted.

"Green Blade?" Aeneas gasped with surprise. "Thought you all perished in Mystra after the city fell? Whole Order was wiped out from what I remember. Yet, here you stand."

Dresden pondered for a moment and thought about how to respond. The truth was hard to revisit and he was disappointed by the sinking feeling that it gave him after all these years. "Yeah, here I stand." Dresden shifted the conversation, "What about you?"

"Me? Oh, I have to head back to the Ark with the rest of the Harvesters. Not too sure about how they will react to all this when I tell em. But, that's something we'll have to see. In any case, it's time for me to go. If I see you around, I'm hoping the circumstances are just as interesting."

After Aeneas and his men left, Dresden stopped by to check on Mira before he went his own way. She wasn't overly excited by the events that happened in the cavern. She was shown a vision by Karahia, but never decided to share it. The betrayal she felt by Alexander's decision to almost end the world also weighed on her mind.

"He was supposed to be better than us. Save us. And he almost ended us," she said after a moment of silence between her and Dresden.

"Guess it's true that not all the old stories are to be believed. Alex wasn't a bad kid, he had a lot of emotions to deal with, not to mention that so-called *curse* wasn't making his head any clearer."

"Still though, my father believed in them. He taught me to believe that they were the saviors of the world, true guardians."

"Well he was right in a way. Look up, the sky seems to be clearing. All thanks to Alex. Real question is what are you going to do with this new outlook?"

"Take Ostro back to his people, hope to get some kind of land out of it far away from this madness in Acropoli. If not, then just continue on my way."

"I wish you luck, Mira."

"For you, as well. I hope you find your way in this life."

Dresden chuckled as he stood to leave. "I'll see where the way takes me."

In the distant hills, a wounded and exhausted Alexander traversed a wilderness that appeared to be peppered with signs of returning life. Behind him the incessant hum and ominous glow of an open portal abruptly went silent and dark. He did not notice the portal's closure; he did not care. The weary Warden passed several badly ruined statues without notice as he followed an old cobblestone path. Stripped of his sword and shield, he only had his damaged armor to protect himself in the world.

Alexander had changed. Physically, his face was worn by a layer of dirt and scars, and his eyes appeared much older, as though they'd seen a thousand lifetimes of stories that were impossible to put into words. Whatever happened to him, wherever the portal took him, how long he was kept there, it had left an impact on the Warden.

At the end of the cobblestone path was a clearing that led to a familiar cliff, once the sight of many phantoms. Without a thought or hesitation, he continued to the end of the cliff and gazed at the familiar horizon. There he saw the once dreary gray world of dense forests with a mighty river cutting through it become consumed by the glow of a sunrise over the distant mountains. As he stared off into the world ahead of him, Alexander took a deep breath.

"A new world, begins."

As he gazed out, an ominous sensation stirred within Alexander. His hands began to burn.